IN THE SHADOW OF THE PINES

• • •

KAREN K NEWELL

Learn For Your Life Publishing
Camp Hill, PA

About the Cover: Cover Design by Christy Mayeski.
The school photo on the back of the cover is
Alfred Bobbitt's school picture taken about 1935.

ISBN: 1456320882
ISBN-13: 9781456320881

"Sergeant," bellowed the voice of a captain, muffled by the sound of jets flying overhead.

"Yes, Captain," came the calm voice of a young, dark haired airman. He was standing at the opening of a metal warehouse at the end of a runway, clipboard in hand. Once he signed the checklist, the C-54 would be loaded with the crates he had just inspected. An Air Force pilot was waiting nearby, ready to take off.

"Sergeant, what are these boxes of chocolate bars doing here?" demanded the captain. "I specifically ordered that candy was no longer to be included in the supplies we drop from the air."

"Just following orders, Sir. General Tunner stated we are to drop candy bars as part of our mission."

"What!" yelled the red-faced officer. "Are you trying to tell me that thousands of American men lost their lives fighting Hitler and his army, just so we could send *candy bars* to them now?"

"That's a political matter, Sir. It was President Truman that ordered food and supplies dropped to the people in Germany. We're just following orders."

"Yeah, yeah" responded the captain. "They created the United States Air Force as a new branch of the military to give us air superiority if there is ever another world war like the one we just finished. Then what do they have us do? Drop food and supplies to the enemies we defeated! Does that sound like a good use of military planes and weapons to you?"

The young sergeant didn't respond.

"And now," continued the officer's tirade, "we're dropping chocolate bars for the little kids below. Ain't that sweet? I bet you didn't join the military so you could give out candy to hungry little homeless orphans, now, did you, Sergeant?"

For the first time, a fiery spark appeared in the younger man's eyes. "With all due respect, Sir," he replied, "I *was* one."

CHAPTER ONE

The Old Homestead

"Alfred! Prentice! Ya' all need to hurry up!"

The two brothers heard Velma's voice carry to the back shed where they were milking the family goat. Velma had risen early and had already finished her chores of feeding the chickens and gathering the eggs before helping Mama with breakfast. Her voice sounded excited.

"Hurry up, you two slow pokes. We'll be going shortly and Mama still needs help inside," Velma reminded them. She was herding the younger children toward the water pump in the yard to get cleaned up.

The boys rushed to finish their chores and crossed the yard. Papa was carrying shovels to their old family wagon, walking quickly with his long strides. He was humming as he loaded up the family cart.

Papa's excitement was contagious. Even little Billy, still in diapers, seemed eager to climb into the wagon before his older sister had him ready in his patched hand-me-downs. Everyone in the family was excited.

Well, almost everyone. Alfred noticed his mother's drooping shoulders and heard her sigh as she carried a basket she had just packed. "Why isn't Mama excited about the get-together at Grandpa Bud's house?" he wondered. "It's the very best part of the whole year."

The family climbed into a wooden wagon pulled by two mules which would take them first to church and then to their grandfather's farm. August 1935 was a hot month, hot even for Texas. They fanned themselves as the cart started down the road.

"Farm to Market Road 1751" was the full name of the rough country road the family traveled anytime they went anywhere. It was a ten mile stretch of country road in San Augustine County that went right through the middle of the Bobbitt Farm a few miles from the small town of Pineland, Texas. It was simply called FM 1751 by everyone in the area. No one else knew it was there.

As the mules pulled the wagon down the familiar wooded road, the younger children listened as the older siblings described the long-anticipated reunion.

"After church is out, we'll go to the family cemetery down yonder," Alfred explained. "It's a tradition that all the relatives get together every year and put the graveyard in good order."

"And afterwards," Velma continued," we all go over to Grandpa Bud's and Miss Annie's house. And there arc lots of aunts and uncles and cousins. It's kind-of-like we do every Sunday. But it's much bigger 'cuz some of our relatives travel for hours to come to the reunion."

"I'm sure glad we don't have a long ways to travel," added Prentice. "Why would we? We live right here on the Bobbitt Farm with Grandpa's house just on the other side of FM 1751 from our place."

"Yep," agreed Velma. "And with all the aunts and uncles coming, there'll be heaps of food too."

Little eyes widened at the mention of food. They tried to picture plates and plates of food with everyone getting all they wanted to eat.

"Ain't nothing like it was before this dog-gone Depression," said Papa who had overheard part of the discussion. "A man can barely get enough food for each day. These get-togethers ain't like they were before when every family would bring baskets of food and we'd share all day long."

No, life wasn't like it had been before the Depression – the children all knew that. Chores started at a young age and an early hour. Food was scarce, and desserts even more rare. Why just last night they could smell Mama's apple pie baking which made their hungry bellies growl even louder.

"But there'll be some mighty good eatin' anyway," their father continued. "I can taste your Mama's pie already. Right, Esper?"

"Yes," their mother replied quietly. "I just hope there won't be any kind of trouble."

"I ain't gonna put up with nothing," their father started to growl. Mama nudged him quickly.

Alfred and Prentice exchanged questioning glances. "What kind of trouble could there be?" Alfred wanted to ask. But Velma shook her head, silently warning him to say nothing.

The wagon pulled into the yard of the Baptist Missionary Church and the family joined other neighbors already there.

They seated themselves just as the service started.

Alfred sat near the end of the row. Nine years old, he was the oldest son and was expected to help take care of the family. Even now, he looked over at his brothers and sisters seated near him.

Prentice was on one side of him. Just two years younger than Alfred, Prentice looked surprisingly like him though a little shorter. "Could mistake 'em for twins," people often said as they eyed the two boys.

Velma sat on the other side, her hair neatly braided in two pig tails. She was two years older than Alfred, and becoming tall like their mother.

Kenneth was sitting on the other side of Velma. Alfred shook his head. Kenneth's finger nails were dirty. Mama would not like to see that. Their clothes were poor and they went barefoot but they were always neat and clean. Kenneth, however, preferred to be outside with the animals or digging in the dirt.

On the other side of Kenneth sat three year old Mary Joy. She had Mama and Velma's dark hair. "Pert little one," Grandpa had called her. For a young one she could be quite verbal. Alfred smiled as he thought of her standing with her hands on her hips scolding Billy this morning.

Billy was squirming on Mama's lap. She lovingly ran her hand across his back. Billy had a hair lip, making it hard for anyone to understand what he said. But Mama always knew what he was saying.

When Billy was born the doctor said it was a cleft palate. Surgery could be done, but his mouth would always be deformed. Mama had made up her mind then that she would love Billy so very much that all the comments and looks from others would never hurt him. But she also knew in her heart that she could not protect him forever.

Finally the service was over and they stood to sing the final hymn. Mama stood taller than all the other women there. She was even an inch or so taller than Papa who was a good sized man himself. "Tall and strong like a pine tree, your mother is," Papa had said.

In addition to their tall height, Mama and Papa both had near-black hair and darker than average skin. They both were one-fourth Native American, but from different tribes. Their dark hair and complexions were evident in the line of children following them out of the church.

"Hey Fonzie," a neighboring farmer called to Papa. "G' morning, Esper," he nodded to Mama, "How's the family today?"

Alfred groaned inside. He wanted to grab the hands of the younger children and dash to their wagon. Was Papa going to visit with everyone *today*?

"Always be neighborly-like," his father had once said when he punished Alfred for not saying "Howdy" when a neighbor passed. But even Papa cut his visiting short today.

❦

The family cemetery was on the east side of FM 1751. When Alfronzo and Esper and their six children pulled in, dozens of others were already there. Before the children had all scrambled from the wagon they were hugged by aunts and tagged by cousins. Uncles shook hands and slapped others on the back. Papa joined right into the fray, but Mama stayed close to their wagon.

"Not as many as there used to be," noted Uncle John. "People just can't afford to travel like they did before."

Quickly, the men and boys were organized into working teams, while the women and girls headed off the short distance to Grandpa's home. Alfred joined a group that raked the graves to clear up the debris of dried leaves and dead twigs that had fallen since last year. Prentice helped two uncles set straight some old headstones that were leaning over. Papa was mending the fence.

Alfred remembered when he was younger and thought the cemetery was a little scary. "Nonsense," his grandfather had told him then. "Grave yards aren't about death. They're about life."

"You didn't just come out of the pine trees," he was told. "You came from a family. That's what these graves are about. Family. Every one of 'em buried here were part of our family - young 'uns, old ones, all of 'em. These are the ones that made us who we are."

Now that he was older, Alfred understood more of what his Grandpa Bud had meant. His father and uncles weren't disturbed by the cemetery. He listened to their happy voices as they mended the fence and tended the headstones. They talked and laughed as they worked, recounting stories about relatives they had known when they were young.

Alfred noticcd that his father's voice was no longer laughing with the others. He glanced over and saw Papa looking at one small tombstone, newer than many of the others. The inscription stated, "Elmer Bobbitt, Our Little Darling, 1922 – 1924."

Alfred had never known the two year old girl who was his older sister. She had died before Velma was born.

"It would seem strange," Alfred reflected, "to have another sister even older than Velma. I wonder what she would have been like."

But as he continued clearing pine needles around the base of one very old tombstone, he looked up and gasped. "Alfonzo Iza Bobbitt, 1866-1873" the stone read. Why that was his father's name! But Papa wasn't dead!

"He was my little brother," said a dccp voice behind Alfred. He felt a firm but kind hand on his shoulder, and knew before he even looked up it was his grandfather who had spoken.

"But - that's my father's name," Alfred stammered.

"Yes, it is," replied his grandfather. "And it was the name of my brother, too. But neither of them were the first Alfonzo Iza Bobbitt. In fact, there's some real history behind that name."

"You see, my father - he's the one we often call "Aug" – why he came out to Texas in 1846 from Mississippi. You wanna know why he came out here? Aug had a brother named, 'Alfonzo Iza Bobbitt' – same name as you see on this tombstone, but it was a different Alfonzo. This first Alfonzo was actually my uncle. And he was a sheriff back in Mississippi."

"Wow, a real sheriff with a gun?" asked Prentice who had wandered over to listen to his grandfather's story.

"Yep, a real shootin' sheriff," continued Grandpa Bud. "But a sheriff has his enemies too. One day when Alfonzo was running for re-election he was giving a speech. Must have been saying something his opponent didn't like, because the other man grabbed a big Bowie knife and tried to stab Alfonzo with it. Fortunately for Alfonzo, Aug was there, and when he saw the man taking a knife to his brother, well he just reached for his gun and 'bang' – shot him.

"Well, Aug saved his brother from getting killed, but now he had other problems. He was worried that he was gonna be hung for shooting the other man. So he left Mississippi and high-tailed it out here to Texas, figuring nobody would find him way out here. Wasn't a lot of people in these parts back then. Many of 'em that were here were traders, and Indians, and outlaws. There were also law-abiding citizens who came to Texas for a chance for a new life on wide open land.

"So Aug came out here, got married to my mother, and settled down in these pine woods of East Texas. It was some time after that he found out that the man he shot didn't die after all. But since he was already settled here he just stayed put.

"Years later, Aug heard that my Uncle Alfonzo had died. That same year my little brother was born, so Aug named him Alfonzo after the brother he had left in Mississippi almost thirty years before. That second Alfonzo is this little boy whose grave you was just cleaning up. He was one of the nine children in my family.

"Five years younger than me," continued their grandfather in a quiet and distant voice. "Always happy, always asking questions, he was. Liked to follow Old Aug around, and when he couldn't find him, he'd just follow me instead."

"One day he was helpin' on our farm not far from here. Had an accident which took his life. That was a sad day I'll never forget. Aug took it real hard. It was the first of his children to die. He wanted his son to be buried close by so they buried him right on this land. Yes sir, his was the very first grave here. Of course, as time went on other family members passed away, as always happens, and this here land became our family cemetery."

"That's sad," said seven year old Prentice. He was contemplating the grave of the seven year old child who would have been his great-uncle.

"Yes, it certainly was sad for Grandpa Aug and Grandma Martha and all of us at the time. But every generation comes 'n goes. Time just doesn't stand still, for Aug, or Little Alfonzo, or any of us. But that doesn't mean people forget. I never forgot. So when your own pa was born, I named him after my brother Alfonzo. So your pa is actually the third boy in the family with the name Alfonzo Iza."

"And Prent and I are named after Papa," chimed Alfred.

"That's right," their Uncle Clarence spoke up. He was straightening a near-by gravestone and listening to his father's speech. "When he named the two of you 'Alfred Fonzio' and 'Alvy Prentice' your father was carrying on the old name. Ha, and the size of crew he's got, I know your Pa won't go to the grave childless like this Little Alfonzo. Huh, boy?"

Chuckles from other relatives encouraged Uncle Clarence's teasing. There was always so much to learn at the reunions. Some of it was funny, and some of it was sad. But all of it was interesting, Alfred thought.

Some of the cousins and uncles were assigned the task of repairing ATL Bobbitt Senior's grave. This was the great-grandfather that people often called "Old Aug." He was the father of Little Alfonzo and Grandpa Bud. In fact, he was the father, grandfather, or great-grandfather of everyone buried in the cemetery.

There were lots of stories and rumors about the old family patriarch. As a result, treasure hunters frequently dug up the grave looking for gold. It often upset Alfred to see the old man's grave disturbed again.

"Confounded grave diggers," said one uncle. "Of course, old Granddaddy Aug didn't take gold to his grave. That rumor was a bunch of hogwash."

"Oh no it weren't," declared another. "My pa was there when Grandpa Aug died, and I swear it's the truth that Grandpa was trying to tell 'em all where he buried his gold as he lay dying on his bed, less'n a mile from here."

"Yeah, he made motions all right," replied another, "but who's to tell what he was trying to say since he couldn't talk. Might as well have been telling us where he hid his chicken bones."

"I've heard others say he was rich 'cuz of all this land he owned. If he was rich he might 'uv wanted to tell where his gold was. "Specially since no one else found any o' his riches after he died," said the first.

"That's cuz there weren't no gold," injected the skeptic. "When he died in 1909 no one in these parts had any extra gold. The only thing he owned was this very land, and that sure don't make nobody rich."

Alfred thought his own father's explanation was the best. "Naw, times were hard after the Civil War," he said. "If old Grandpa had had any gold, he would have needed it to buy food and farm tools. Don't make no sense that he would have buried his gold, lived real poor-like after that, and then waited 'til he couldn't even talk no more to tell where his gold was. Any gold he'd ever had was spent long before 1909."

"Anyway, his grave and many other a place on this homestead has been dug up by people looking for that gold," said Uncle Clarence. "One thing's certain. He sure couldn't 'uv put it in his own coffin with him. I wish people would just let him rest in peace."

Debating old rumors appeared to be a regular part of the family reunion. But now with Great-grandfather Aug's grave restored, as well as the rest of the cemetery, the workers started to get ready to head towards the homestead house.

"You boys can go on over with the others," said their father. "I'm gonna take the tools and wagon and mules back to our house and will be back with the rest of ya'all in a few minutes."

☙❧

The men and boys joined the women and girls at Grandpa's house. The children stared in wonder at the tables. Doors were placed across old saw horses to create tables. Anything that wasn't nailed down was made into a table top and loaded with food. There were tables in the living room and outside on the lawn. Alfred went into the dog run and saw there were more tables there.

Grandpa Bud's house was a large double-cabin with a dog run going down the middle, similar to the house where Alfred and his family lived. Made of bare wooden planks, it was actually two cabins with a fifteen foot open dog run in between. One roof covered both cabins and the dog run, making a single dwelling out of it. Doors from both cabins opened into the dog run so one could easily get from one part of the house to the other. A long porch stretched 60 feet across the front of both cabins.

Alfred chose to sit at one of the homemade tables in the dog run. Both dogs and humans enjoyed the shade and the breeze between the two cabins. The children liked the dog run because one could be indoors and outdoors at the same time.

Prentice brought his plate and sat across from Alfred. Cousins and uncles joined them. Most greeted the brothers quite warmly. But, Alfred noticed, some seemed more distant, as if they didn't quite know what to say to them. "Did we do something wrong," he wondered?

But nothing could diminish his pleasure at the plateful of food in front of him.

"I've never seen so much food before," Prentice mumbled between bites.

"But just isn't like it was in the old days," one cantankerous uncle grumbled. "Back then we had some real good food."

Almost 100 people were there, the grandchildren or great-grandchildren of ATL Bobbitt Sr. - the "Old Aug" of Grandpa Bud's stories. That meant they were either the children of Grandpa Bud or the children of his brothers and sisters. His grandfather's eyes sparkled as he went from table to table greeting everyone who had come.

Alfred's eyes shone as he watched his grandfather. He loved the tall old man with his Welsh-Irish complexion and white beard. Alfred was proud that he and his family lived on this homestead. But they lived in a different house on the other side of FM 1751, a few miles away from Grandpa's and Miss Annie's home.

Miss Annie was Grandpa's wife, but not their grandmother. Their real grandmother, who was their Papa's mother, had died about fifteen years ago. Later Grandpa had married Miss Annie.

Alfred noticed his own father was also mingling and visiting with others. His mother, however, had stayed behind, helping in Miss Annie's kitchen. "Why is she avoiding everyone?" her son wondered.

Children quickly gulped down their food and rushed to play with their cousins. Alfred and Prentice found themselves the center of attention when Prentice pulled an Indian arrow head from his pocket.

"Wow! Look what Prent has," called one boy.

"What is it? What do you have?"

"Just an old Indian arrow head," replied Prentice, as boys gathered in a circle around him.

"Where did ya get that?"

"Alfred gave it to me," was the answer.

"We get 'em all the time up on that hill," Alfred explained, pointing to the slope behind Grandpa's house. "After a heavy rain, they just about wash right up under our feet."

"Where? Show us," excited voices clamored.

Alfred and Prentice led the way up the back hill between their grandfather's house and Bobbitt Creek. A posse of boys scavenged the area, looking for the cherished arrow heads. A holler was heard whenever one was found.

The Indian arrow heads seemed like treasure even more valuable than Grandfather Aug's gold. "Well, it certainly is much more plentiful than any gold I've ever seen 'round these parts," thought Alfred.

After the kids grew tired of treasure hunting, they raced back to the homestead to show their finds to any interested adults. Grandpa Bud, of course, was always interested.

"Tell us how the Indian arrow heads got there, Grandpa," one child requested. "Yes, tell us," others pleaded. Grandfather was a good story teller.

As Grandpa made his way onto the living room hearth, a semi-circle of children gathered around. "Well ya see, a long time ago, there were no white people on this land. Even before Mexico owned Texas, this land was settled by the Indians. And out back there," he pointed to the hill north of his house, "was an Indian encampment of the Kadohadacho Indians. We just call them the Caddo Indians now."

"Were they mean? Did they scalp people?" young voices inquired.

"Oh no. They were quite friendly. In fact, that is how Texas got its name. When the French came over and met these natives, they called them "Friendly Indians," or Tejas

Indians in the French language. With time, that got changed to Texas. However, the Indians continued to call themselves by their rightful name: Kadohadacho. Caddo, for short. They were farmers, they were. Not much need for scalpin' anybody."

"Did the Indians give you this land, Grandpa?"

"No, not exactly. Your Grandma Lizzie was part Indian ya' know, but she wasn't from the Caddo tribe. Nope, her mother Jerusha was from one of the Eastern tribes. But it was my grandparents who were given this land from the Mexican government.

Texas used to be part of Mexico, ya know. Back in 1835 – that was a year before the Alamo - my grandfather, Joses Hoby, was granted one Spanish league of land under the Zavalla Colony.

"Was your grandfather Mexican?"

"Oh no, he was from North Carolina. Back then North Carolina was considered a civilized place, and Texas was more frontierlike. Grandpa took up with a girl, you see, and both families were against it. So you know what they did? They got married anyway and ran off to Texas. "GTT" was what they used to write in the books - "Gone to Texas." Since he and his new wife Lizette wanted to settle on this land, the Mexican government granted them this league.

"Oh life out here was hard for Joses and Lizette, let me tell you. They were not only ranchers and pioneers, but he was in the Texas militia. This land went from being under the Mexican government, to being the independent Republic of Texas, to becoming one of the states in the United States of America. And at that time trouble was really brewing between the North and the South over slavery. All that and them tryin' to raise ten kids besides.

When they died, they divided up their land and left 225 acres to their daughter, Martha Hobdy Bobbitt. She was my mother. So she and my father, Aug, farmed this land.

Aug's real name was Augustus Tentamous Lafamous Bobbitt. Ha! Just try spelling that, would ya? Well, actually not only did he have to spell it, but I had to too, because that's my name as well. Sometimes they refer to him as ATL Senior, and me as ATL Junior. But "Aug" and "Bud" are what most people call us."

The older kids nodded in understanding when old Grandpa Aug's name was mentioned. He had been a Confederate soldier in the Civil War, and the subject of a number of Grandpa Bud's stories. He was a true war hero, the kids all believed, even if he had been demoted for going AWOL at one point in the war. "A real character," people called Old Aug.

Some stories were funny: like a mail order bride who left town when she saw him in a store. Apparently Aug had led her to believe he was a young man in his letter, even though he was an older widower by then. When the store owner pointed Aug out to her behind his back, the would-be-bride left the store without speaking to him, got on the next train, and never came back.

"Well, when my parents started to homestead this land," Grandpa continued, "it became known as the Bobbitt Farm. And so it is today. I was born in a log house not two hundred feet from here. But with thirteen kids, I needed something bigger 'n a log cabin. So I built this here dog-run house. It was a common type of house in Texas in the 1800's. The dog run provides shade and a good breeze. So your Grandma Lizzie, that was my first wife, she and I built this here house about 30 years ago."

Miss Annie came into the room and did not look happy that Grandpa was talking about the farm and his first wife. Alfred didn't understand why. They always loved hearing about the Bobbitt Homestead. But oftentimes it made adults in the group cranky-like.

"Well, are ya all just gonna sit there a yammering," interrupted Miss Annie, "or do you wanna see the toy room?" She dangled some keys in her hand. Kids jumped up with yelps of agreement. But now it was Grandpa's turn to look unhappy.

At every family reunion that Alfred could remember, Miss Annie let the children go into the toy room for a few minutes. On the north side of Grandpa Bud's house was a room that was always kept locked except for the brief tour every year. When his own children were growing up, it had been the bedroom for one of his sons. When he had died, Grandpa Bud and his wife Lizzie grieved. They just locked the door with the child's toys and furniture still in it.

Over the years, four of Grandpa Bud's children had died and their belongings were added to the room. Some of them were only babies. Going into that room made Alfred feel as if he had stepped into the past.

Eagerly, the kids followed Miss Annie. Grandpa Bud never came along. The door was unlocked and the children filed single-file into the room. Alfred remembered the row of children's graves. It was one thing to see the tombstones and hear stories of long-deceased children. But it was different to see the wagons, and tricycles, and dolls they had played with. It made their lives seem more real.

The cousins looked longingly at toys that had been made for other children years before. Toys were a luxury few of them had. "You can look, but don't touch," said Miss Annie. As tempting as it might be to sit on one of the riding toys, they knew they dare not ask.

After the toy tour ended, the small herd of children wandered back to the living room where another family tradition was taking place: the debate on politics. Family political debates could range from friendly ribbing to near-duels.

But the last few years there was only one topic and no one disagreed. The economy was bad. Every child there knew quite well the economy was bad - even if he or she had no idea what an economy was. The reason the economy was bad, however, was still a topic the uncles would debate.

"It's the Yankees that started this Depression. Ever since the Civil War they've been bent on destroying us."

"Ah, get off. The Yankees got it just as bad as we do – and probably deserve it, mind you. But their crops have been failing all the time that ours has been."

"It's not just us and the Yankees," interjected a third voice. There's been economic troubles all over the world. A global depression, they say."

"Well, at least Washington is doin' a something about it, though it took 'em long enough. They've got new programs to help people get work."

"Welfare, that's what that is," scoffed an indignant uncle. "No self respecting man would accept that money. Why, I'd just as soon starve and see my kids starve too before I'd take one cent of that communist money."

"And some has no choice," retorted another. "And whether you'd take it or not, I said it's high time those up in government did something about it."

"You don't understand finance, that's the problem with too many of your generation. Why it's those very same programs that's a causing this bad economy to drag on and on. That's why the other nations in the world are recovering from this here Depression faster 'en we are."

"No, no, no. It's the Yankees I tell you. Can't just win a war, they need to see if they can starve us, and our kids, and grandkids, and great-grand kids too."

The animated debate continued. They agreed the economy was bad. But that was just about all you could get a roomful of relatives to agree on.

Fortunately a happier sound greeted their ears. From the parlor came the sound of Aunt Lou playing the piano. Those tired of the political debate – and those who had no interest in it in the first place - gathered round the old piano. "She'll be coming round the mountain when she comes," sang a chorus of happy voices.

Alfred was drawn to the music. He didn't necessarily understand the words to all the songs any more than he did the political debates, but the music certainly was more upbeat. His mother had left the kitchen and was across the room from him, singing too. She looked at him and smiled. He heard his grandfather's deep voice and turned towards him. Grandpa Bud winked at him.

"This is what it means to be family," thought Alfred. "Whether the economy is bad or not, we still belong to each other." He looked back and forth between his mother and grandfather – two people he loved dearly. Why would they not look at each other? Was he imagining it?

The singing continued. After a while, Alfred noticed some of the older boys motioning to each other, and slipping out of the room one by one. Curious, Alfred joined them outside. "We're gonna have a wasp fight," he was told.

Alfred's face lit up with anticipation. Wasp fights were exciting, and even somewhat practical. Every farm had trouble with pesky wasps. They built their strong nests in the eves of houses and made sitting or playing on a porch a bit precarious at times. And Grandpa Bud's house had a long porch that went straight across the entire front length of the house, where several wasp nests might be hanging at any one time. The kids, however, had their revenge through the great wasp fights.

"Okay, we gotta form teams," Ray, one of his older cousins, was saying.

The boys quickly grouped themselves into three teams. Alfred was delighted that they considered him old enough to be on one of the teams now. He was in the group that Ray was leading.

"Remember," Ray was coaching the group, "we not only have to knock the nests down, but we gotta out run 'em too. They'll be madder than mad when their nests fall, and let me tell you their stingers really hurt!"

The group leaders broke off from the others to scout the area and plan the angles of attack and escape. Meanwhile the others were gathering sticks, small rocks, old horse shoes – anything that could be thrown at the nests to knock them down.

The kids kept their plans away from Grandpa Bud. His youngest son, Elijah, whose toys the children had just seen on the toy tour had died because of a wasp fight. He had suffered a head injury when a hurled rock missed the wasp nest and hit him instead. Best to let Grandpa in on the plans *after* the attack was finished.

"Listen up now," Ray called to his group after the older boys had finished their battle plans. "We're gonna do that nest there in the middle first. Then the one to the right. They are both red wasps. We'll save that big nest in the corner for last. It's got black wasps."

The experienced boys knew the red wasps could be more easily tricked than the black wasps. With good timing, one would drop to the ground and the red wasps would fly over the invader.

But the black wasps were different. They were meaner and faster and could often overtake the would-be escapee who was likely to have some pretty nasty stings as war injuries. Experience had taught them it was better to save the black wasps for last.

More cousins were joining the boys. Even a few girls joined the teams. Most of the girls, including Velma, preferred to watch from a distance. They also kept the small children from getting stung by angry wasps or trampled by their fleeing attackers.

"Ready!" yelled one of the leaders as the boys picked up their weapons.

"Aim!"

Alfred drew back his arm, focusing on the nest in the middle.

"Fire!"

Dozens of stones, sticks, rotten apples, and other miscellaneous items soared through the air, many of them striking the middle wasp nest. The nest was shaken, but stayed on the roof. Dozens of wasps flew out in all directions.

Alfred turned and ran as quick as he could. "Drop, drop," he could hear Velma yelling. He fell to the ground as several red wasps flew over him. Around him, he could hear other cousins doing the same.

The wasp nest was loose, but it was still hanging. Ray grabbed a big, long stick and quickly strode over to the porch. He swung it forcefully, batting the nest off the porch roof. The nest flew through the air, and landed near Alfred. With a yelp, he scrambled to his feet and tore off towards a group of pine trees. Others nearby were also shrieking and fighting to get away.

Alfred ran right into Velma and Kenneth as he dashed away from the nest. They were cheering and laughing with all the other spectators. The nest was down and no one had been stung.

"Do it again. Let's do it again," excited voices shouted.

Once again, the warriors stocked up on weapons of destruction. They picked the next target and gathered around it. The ring of spectators crept closer.

"Ready, aim, fire!" came the familiar command. Again, a shower of missiles was launched towards the porch, this time knocking down the nest with the first bombardment. As the angry wasps swarmed from their nests, the attackers turned and fled in opposite directions.

In the middle of all the yells and laughter, Alfred heard a wail. He turned to see little Kenneth lying on the ground with one of his older cousins on top of him. "I wanted to see the wasps," he sobbed in answer to the scolding. Velma and Alfred lifted him up.

"Just a few scratches, no stings," Velma announced.

Alfred reminded the little ones to stay further away, and once again joined the older boys gathering close to the porch again.

"Okay, this is gonna be harder. Now we gotta get that black wasp nest," one of the other leaders was saying as Alfred returned towards the porch.

In order to outsmart the more dangerous black wasps, the groups stationed themselves at different angles. "That group is going to attack first," Ray said as he pointed to the crew on his left. We have to keep crouched to the ground. When the wasps are chasing them, then we charge. We throw at the hive *and* the wasps from a different direction.

It confuses them. Then as we are running away, that group over there throws their rocks. That oughta knock the nest down and completely confuse them."

"Remember, ya'll have to run fast and long. These wasps are fast, smart, and mean. If you drop to the ground, they won't fly over ya. You'll get stung. Everyone understand?"

Prentice had joined Alfred, and they both crouched to the ground with the others in their team, waiting for their signal. They didn't have long to wait. The first leader shouted, "Fire", and objects were hurled through the air from the first group.

"Now" shouted Ray as Alfred's group jumped up and began to launch their weapons from a different angle. As soon as he had let his rock fly, Alfred turned to run. He stopped for just an instant to grab Prentice's hand and drag him along.

"Run, run," Alfred urged his brother.

Even as they were running across the yard, Alfred heard an agonizing yell. It was Ray. He was stung in the neck.

But there was not a moment's pause. The third team was up and throwing the last assortment of missiles. Some threw them at the wasp nest which was now falling, and others threw them at the cloud of enraged wasps. All the attackers were running; the spectators all yelling.

In the midst of the commotion, a loud shriek was heard, followed by a high pitch wail. One of the younger attackers had been stung on the cheek. As the swarm of wasps disappeared, the girls gathered around the sobbing victim. Too old to run into the house crying, but too young to curtail his sobs completely, the younger cousin shook from pain as his cheek started to swell.

Ray held back his tears. He grimaced and rubbed his neck, but feared tears more than pain.

Out of the front door strode Grandpa Bud. He kicked the fallen hive sending it soaring across the yard. Quickly he crossed the yard, scooped up his great-nephew in his arms, and headed back to the house without saying a word.

"Ya'all quit your augging around," scolded Aunt Dora who had followed Grandpa out of the house. "Augging around," was a term the Bobbitt children heard when they were bothering the adults. No one outside the family ever used the term.

"It's cuz of old Aug," Dora had told Mama last year. "He was known to play practical jokes and not behave himself."

The wasp fight lasted 45 minutes. In the end, three wasps nests were destroyed, two boys suffered stings, and one child had been trampled. All in all the children felt they had won a fair fight. That is, those who had not been stung thought they had won.

As the shadows lengthened, Alfred noticed Ray across the yard motioning for him to follow. Curious, Alfred walked over towards the shed.

"Let's get some of them apples," Ray suggested as he nodded towards Grandpa's orchard. "No one is looking."

"Can't," replied Alfred. "Miss Annie will catch us. She even knows my foot prints."

"Oh, I'm not scared of Miss Annie," retorted Ray. "Besides, I got an idea."

Ray handed Alfred two scraps of wood he found from the wood pile. Ray took two other scraps and tied them to his bare feet with twine. They were a little like snow shoes. He showed Alfred how to do the same.

"There, Miss Annie will never know who done it."

Looking over their shoulders to make sure no one from the house was watching, the two cousins snuck into the orchard. They grabbed several handfuls of apples and headed back to the shed to eat them.

Alfred felt guilty stealing the fruit. Hadn't they eaten the best feast he could remember? Besides, what were they going to do with the apple cores?

"We'll just dig a little hole right here and bury 'em," said Ray. They dug a hole with their bare hands to hide the evidence. They threw the wood back on the wood pile, tossed the vines behind some branches and walked back around the shed with dirty fingernails and guilty expressions.

There they met Miss Annie, standing and looking at them with her arms crossed. "You boys can't fool me," was all she said.

As the sun was fading and the temperature dropped, Alfred joined other cousins on the front porch. From there, they could hear another debate heating up inside the house. This sounded angrier than the political discussion earlier that day. It sounded as if they were accusing someone. But who?

Alfred caught words of "homesteaders rights," and "share-cropping." His stomach turned. Sometimes the grown-up folks would get very angry – even start yelling – when the subject of land came up.

Velma and Alfred exchanged glances. They could hear their father's irate voice over several others. "Why couldn't people just get along?" Alfred wondered. "Do they have to fight?"

Just then his father stormed out of the house with his mother and the two smallest children behind him. "We're going home; get Prent and Kenneth," he snapped at Velma. "Now!"

Quickly Alfred and Velma rounded up the younger boys. Papa's face was very red; Mama looked as if she was going to cry. The fun day had ended on a sour note. They walked briskly through the woods, crossing the road to get to their farm house. No one said a word.

CHAPTER TWO

Cold and Hungry

Back at their cabin, with the younger three tucked in bed for the night, Mama and Papa sat at the kitchen table and talked. The older three siblings had their own pow-wow to discuss the day's events. Velma joined Alfred and Prentice in the boys' bedroom. They were careful to speak quietly so they didn't wake up Kenneth or Billy.

"Mama and Papa used to have a store and gas station at Blue Springs, a little ways from here," Velma explained to her brothers. "I remember them working late into the evenings when I was little. You were both born there."

The boys nodded in understanding. Alfred had some vague memories of the house before they moved to the farm. Sometimes the children heard their parents talk about the store in the "good old days."

"All of a sudden, the economy got bad. The store closed. And we didn't have a place to live," continued Velma. "Since Grandpa Bud has four houses for sharecroppers on this land, he let us come here and live in this house as sharecroppers."

"What's a sharecropper?" asked Prentice.

"It's like a tenant farmer. Grandpa owns all this land, but he lets the sharecroppers come in and live on the land. He gives them the seeds, and the animals, and the tools. Then the sharecropper does the work," Velma explained.

"Grandpa used to do all the work of running the farm himself," Alfred offered "But now that he is older he has sharecroppers doing much of it for him."

"That's right," Velma responded. "Then when the harvest comes each year, the sharecropper keeps half of what he produced, and gives the other half to the landowner. That's Grandpa. That's how sharecropping works. And that's why we live here on Grandpa's land and the other aunts and uncles don't."

"Why do people get mad at us for being sharecroppers?" asked Alfred. "Did you notice that some of the uncles weren't as friendly to us as they used to be?"

"The first two years we lived here, Mama and Papa planted the seeds Grandpa gave him. They also took care of the herd of cattle. But Papa also did other work when he could find it. He used our wagon to take kids to school who lived too far from the school house to walk. That money bought the seeds to plant crops and to buy his own farm tools. So we aren't really sharecroppers anymore – at least that's what Papa says. So, when Grandpa Bud came to get his half of the produce last year, Mama and Papa wouldn't give it to him. They said it was theirs because they bought the seeds and animals themselves. "

"I was helping in the kitchen when I overheard Aunt Dora and Aunt Lou talking," Velma said, dropping her voice to a whisper. The boys leaned closer to hear.

"They said they don't like Miss Annie much, and they wish Grandpa Bud had never married her. They said Grandpa wouldn't care much about our crops and all since we're his grandkids, but Miss Annie demands he collect all the crops from all four of the sharecroppers, including us. I heard 'em say that she is just looking out for herself."

"But there is more to it" Alfred added. "Papa says that part of this land we are farming does belong to him, 'cuz his mama died and left it to him."

"She left all the land to Papa?" Prentice asked.

"No, not all of it. Grandpa had nine kids, so Papa would own one ninth of it." Alfred drew an imaginary box with his finger on the bed, and tried to show how to divide it into nine pieces.

"He actually owns even more," responded Velma. "Whenever he goes away to build a bridge, he gets some money. And Mama said he has bought land from his brothers and sisters when they would sell it to him."

"That's right," confirmed Alfred. "One dollar an acre - that is what the land cost him. And he has bought 68 acres. He told me that."

Prentice whistled. "Sixty eight dollars! Wow, that's a lot of money."

The three were quiet for a minute, thinking how much money their father had spent buying land. Sixty eight dollars would buy a lot of food.

"He's built a lot of bridges and done a lot of work to earn that money," Velma reflected. "So, Papa says the land is his since he bought it. And he bought the seeds and animals, so the harvest is his. But some of the aunts and uncles say that the land isn't his while Grandpa Bud is living. Grandpa Bud was farming this land before we came here as sharecroppers and according to homesteading rights you can't take the land away from a homesteader just because their wife dies."

"So who is right? Grandpa or Papa?"

"I don't know."

❧

After the others went to bed, Alfred lay in the dark thinking. Who was right? Was Papa a thief who was stealing crops and lands from Grandpa? Couldn't be. Was their kind old grandfather taking advantage of their family by trying to take crops from them when they had bought the land, the seeds, and done all the work? It didn't make any sense.

Alfred sighed. Sometimes it was easy to know who the bad guys were and who the good guys were. Like the Yankees and

Confederates. Everyone knew the Yankees were bad. All four of Alfred's great-grandfathers had been Confederate soldiers so there could be no arguing that point.

But what about a family land dispute. Were they the bad guys? Was Grandpa Bud ?

What about what Velma had overheard their aunts saying about Miss Annie? "She's just looking out for herself," they had said.

But why shouldn't she? Was there anything wrong with her looking out for herself? She was good to Grandpa and worked hard on his farm. She might be strict with the boys, but she was also fair. She was a great cook, made the best bacon he'd ever tasted, and was quick to share. She had never made Alfred feel unwelcome in their home.

It was so confusing.

Early the next morning, Alfred went to the shed to milk his goat, Nancy. He milked the other goats at Grandpa's place too. Grandpa had twenty-five goats and he let Alfred milk them and keep the milk for his brothers and sisters. When Nancy was born, the mother goat wouldn't let her nurse so Miss Annie had shown Alfred how to feed her from a bottle. Since he had grown attached to Nancy, Grandpa had let him keep her as his very own.

After taking the fresh goat milk into their kitchen, Alfred went into the field to pick beans. It was a tiring job, and the sun was already starting to make the air extremely hot, even though it was still quite early. But it was better to be hot than to be hungry, Alfred thought.

With his morning chores done, the boy headed over toward his grandfather's house. With all the relatives gone, it was much quieter than it had been yesterday. Alfred welcomed the quiet, and slipped into the dining room where he found Grandpa Bud. His grandfather was sitting at the long

12 foot boarding-house style wooden table. There were two long wooden benches on either side, as well as chairs that actually had arms at both ends of the table. Grandpa always sat on the chair at the west side of the room. Alfred slid onto the bench near him.

His grandfather winked and poured a little of his coffee into the saucer for Alfred to drink. It was one of their secrets. Mama would never approve of her children drinking coffee. Alfred enjoyed the sweet taste of sugar and cow's milk mixed with the coffee. But he had learned as a small lad sitting on his Granddaddy's lap not to ask for more than he was given.

Since Grandpa was a great story teller and loved to have someone listen, Alfred learned all kinds of things. History, particularly Civil War stories, livestock and crops, weather, local legends about neighbors and kin.

"Keep your mouth shut, listen and learn and don't correct your grandfather," Papa had said long ago. It was good advice, and

Alfred had learned lots from obeying it. Today Grandpa told him about the pine trees.

"Gotta chop down a white pine that may be getting close to falling over and collapsing one of our sheds. You know how to tell the difference between a white and yellow pine?"

Alfred shook his head indicating he did not know. But he also knew he was soon to find out.

"Always know your pine trees, boy, especially if you're gonna cut one down. The white pines, they are native to this area. Stronger and taller than the yellow pines, they are. When the settlers first come to this area, they didn't appreciate at first the fine qualities of the white pine. They just saw 'em as giant weeds occupyin' the acres they wanted to use for planting crops. So they just started to chop 'em down.

"Trouble is they started chopping right and left." Grandpa shook his head at the wastefulness of it. 'Tried to use the same farming techniques used back East, but that's a different kind of soil and needs a different kind o' farming. This is timberland, and good timber too, 'specially the white pines. Ya just can't go a chopping 'em all up and then plant the same crops in their place year after year. Don't work that way.

"You need to rotate the crops and the livestock on this here timberland, as I've been showing ya. But the first settlers, they took down the strong white pines and planted the faster growing yellow pines in their place. And shore 'enough, the yellow pines sprang up fast enough in this region. But way too many of the tall white pines is a gone."

They had left the house and were heading over to check out the white pine tree in question. Yes indeed, Alfred noted, it was taller and stronger than the other pine trees. Grandpa showed him how to tell a white pine. Their needles were always set in groups of five.

"Remember that," Grandpa said. "White has five letters: w- h –i – t – e. And it always has five needles at the end of each twig. And don't never go chopping down a white pine without good cause."

But he showed his young learner that this pine was past its prime and no longer putting out the pine cones like the stronger pine trees. Better to cut it down in the direction you wanted it to land, than let it fall on a shed or fence. It might also split the trunk through the middle, if it fell on its own. It would be better to keep a long trunk for a bridge or the beam of a barn.

Alfred heard how the tall trunks had been used as masts in the ship building industries, and way over on the east coast the white pines had all been completely depleted by ship builders who hadn't thought ahead to future generations. "It's here in this timberland that the white pine'll grow again," Grandpa predicted.

Alfred knew every bit of that tree would go to good use and none of it wasted. The tall trunk might become the beam of a barn. Needles and twigs could be used as tender for starting a fire. Knots were used in the cook-stoves. Even pinecones were used for washing dishes. Pine cones could also be used as balls by a generation that had few other toys.

So Grandpa started to lay his plans for chopping down the tree. He would get Papa and one of the other tenant farmers to help him, and Alfred could help too. That reminded Alfred of the land dispute. He looked at his Grandpa but said nothing. He knew that was a topic he was to avoid.

Alfred headed back to his own house, knowing that they would be picking corn in the afternoon. He saw his mother bent over, weeding her large vegetable garden. She stood up, her full height, and called cheerfully to him as he passed. "She's a white pine," her son thought, "tall and strong."

❧❦

Summer days passed quickly. There were weeds to be pulled, hay to be baled, fruit from the orchard to be picked. There were also fences to mend. San Augustine County had open range, which meant all cattle were allowed to roam free – on the owners land or anyone else's. Farmers put up fences not to keep their animals in, but to keep them out of their gardens. Whether they were at their own home or Grandpa's, the three bigger kids kept busy as the hot August days passed.

Alfred liked to help with his grandfather's animals, since they didn't have enough money for livestock of their own. He and Prent would help shear the sheep for their wool, or keep the gates as the different animals came in and out at shearing time. They were amused at the surprised sheep who looked naked after their wool was shorn off. The animals didn't even recognize each other.

The boys went to a hog round up that summer. They cut gashes in the ears of new pigs in a certain manner to identify the owner. That was necessary since a pig was just as likely to forage on a neighbor's land as much as it would its own.

Every month Alfred would join Grandpa and four or five other neighbors who would collectively steer their herds on a cattle drive to have them dipped in a chemical to kill ticks and parasites. Even the cattle were having a hard time in the Depression, and a farmer didn't want to lose any of his precious cows to parasites.

"How do you know which of the cows are yours, Grandpa?" he asked, as he nudged his horse forward, so he could be aside the old man.

"Why Alfred, I'll have to have you come with me to the next branding. Can't you see that mark on their left hip? That's my brand. Most of us just use our initials, but you can use 'most any symbol you want to register – 'long as no one else is usin' it that is."

"But Grandpa," he continued, "Sometimes when we are walking in the woods or the pasture, you know whether the herd belongs to you or someone else before you even see it."

"Yep," his grandfather agreed. "Different size bells make different sounds. I can tell my cows by their bells, by the brands on their hips, sometimes even by the way they moo."

"Yo, there!" called another farmer. "Git back there."

Alfred saw one of the cows break from the herd and dash toward the woods on the side of the road. Instantly, his grandfather and several others were after him. Alfred joined the race, running his horse to try to head the cow off. Just as he expected, it was his grandfather that caught the cow and brought it back. He was the oldest man there, but he always got a cow he was after.

"Was it one of yours?" Alfred asked.

"Nope," was the answer. "And it don't matter none. On these cattle drives we all work together 'til we get 'em all home."

಄಄

Alfred was looking forward to September and the start of school. There was one question that was bothering him though. What would he wear for shoes to school this year?

Every year after the fall harvest was sold, everyone would get a pair of shoes. They usually bought the shoes a little large, because it was the one and only pair they would get all year – and pity the child whose feet grew more than expected. Over the fall and winter months the shoes would be worn to church and school. And usually about the time school was out the next spring, the shoes would be in tatters, or pretty close.

The children didn't mind throwing away their old shoes. Texas summers were quite warm and young feet were soon accustomed to running up and down gravel roads and rocky soil barefoot. Of course, there was always a concern for rattlesnake bites and scorpions, especially in tall grass or layers of pine needles.

Alfred had a few close calls with rattlesnakes over the summer months, and it had taught him to be careful. He hadn't been quite so lucky with scorpions. Neither he nor his siblings would ever forget the awful sting of that lobster-looking insect. But snakes and scorpions withstanding, it was normal to see children barefoot in the summer months.

Since all the crops were not harvested until after school started, sometimes one had to start school without shoes. Since all the farmers in the area were hit with the same economic problems, money was scarce and no one said anything if a student was barefoot. However, Alfred and Velma and Prentice had a long hike to the school yard, and it would be difficult to make that journey barefoot once the colder weather came.

This year Alfred had "grown like a weed," as Mama said. He couldn't get his feet into the old shoes one way or the other. "Prent will have to wear Alfred's shoes from last year. I'll mend 'em up best I can," reflected Mama.

But what would Alfred do?

Farmers kept much of the crops they grew for their own family to use. However they did convert as much as they could to cash. The cash would be used for necessities they could not make themselves: paper, coffee, stamps, salt, medicines - and shoes.

One by one the crops were harvested. "Barely enough, barely enough," Papa kept muttering. There was little that could be sold for cash. And what was sold, brought in very little money in those days of the Depression.

Papa strode into the kitchen and dropped a bag of flour and some spices on the table after he got back from town. "That's all I could buy and it's got to hold us. Robbery," he added, "that's what it is."

"Papa," Velma asked, "are we gonna get new shoes?"

"New shoes!" bellowed her father. "Do I look like a rich man? Don't know why ya' all think ya need new shoes just to sit in the school house all day."

"Your father gets angry when he can't get what you need," Mama had said after Papa had stormed out of the house. "It hurts him and makes him cross."

A few days before school was to start Alfred and Prentice were crossing FM 1751 between Grandpa Bud's cabin and their own. They saw the Watkins Peddler pushing his cart down the road, and they waved their greeting and called "howdy" to him. The peddler's cart contained quite a conglomeration: scissors, pans, medicines, spices, needle and thread. If anyone would buy it, he would carry it.

During the Depression, more people were surviving on the barter system. When you barter for goods, you don't actually use money. A farmer might exchange some eggs for some cloth to make curtains. A person living in town might exchange curtains they had made for some eggs. Of course, the peddler had to get some of the eggs and some of the cloth too. Since so many of the farmers had no cash, the Watkins Peddler Cart had expanded. It now had crates on the side to hold chickens or geese, or hound puppies, or any other item that had been bartered for.

When the boys reached their yard, Mary Joy came skipping up to them. "The peddler was here; the peddler was here," she called. The kids went into the house together and found Mama making lunch in the kitchen. There was an old gunny sack on the table.

The children crowded around the table. Out of the sack came two pairs of shoes, a girl's pair and a boy's pair. They weren't new, but they were still in fairly good condition.

"They fit just great, and room to grow too," chirped Velma as she tried her pair on.

But there was more. She had a pencil for Prentice. He smiled at his mother. With Alfred's outgrown shoes and a pencil, he would now be ready for school too.

Was that it? Was there nothing for the little three? Mama looked at the little ones and pulled out three ripe peaches.

"Holy cow!" Mary Joy exclaimed. Then clapped her hand over her mouth and looked guiltily at Mama. Their mother never tolerated any of her children swearing, and if she heard such talk it earned a "whoopin' from your Pa."

Alfred remembered last year when his mother had overheard forbidden words slip from his mouth. Since their father wasn't around, his mother had taken the sole of her shoe and walloped his behind until it was sore. He never said a bad word after that. But was little Mary Joy going to get spanked now?

"Doesn't seem to matter," Alfred often thought, "that when Papa gets mad he says words we aren't even allowed to *think*."

This time, however, Mama just laughed. "Holy cow, indeed," she answered.

But how had Mama bought all these treasures? Their Papa would never have spent the small amount of hard-earned cash for shoes. Alfred's eyes glanced on the near empty shelf where Mama's canned fruits had been - then he glanced down at the shoes he had just put on moments before. There would be no jam or fruit to eat this winter. But he was happy. He and Velma and Prentice would be ready for school.

☙❧

Besides school, there was another reason Velma, Alfred and Prentice were looking forward to Fall. Grandpa Bud had one of the only sugar cane mills in the area one eighth of a mile north of his house. Friends and neighbors would gather and work together during the long days of the sugar cane harvest.

Mama chose not to go the sugar cane harvest this year. But Velma was eager to go and woke up Alfred and Prentice.

"I wanna to go too," said Kenneth, as the three were starting towards their grandfather's fields. He scrambled behind them as their mother nodded her approval.

Alfred and Prent used cane knives which had curved blades like a machete. They cut down the sugar cane, and took the stalks to feed into the drums. Alfred noticed there was a lot less of the sugar cane stalks this year than in previous years. "This Depression affects everything," Alfred concluded.

Kenneth was proudly leading the mule that turned the drums. Since the mule was tied to the pole turning the drums, all it could do was walk in a circle. As the stalks were squeezed by the turning drums, their juice flowed into wooden barrels.

Velma was working at the copper vat which sloped down-hill from the drums. The vat was a long rectangle, 12 foot by 5 foot, with small sliding gates every twelve inches. Beneath the vat was a stone pit where pine knots were burnt to create a fire to cook the syrup. Velma operated one of the gates in the copper vat that let the syrup move from one part of the vat to the next as it cooked. Experienced women worked at the furthest gates, to make sure the last part of the cooking process was done correctly. It was an art to know the exact moment when the syrup had cooked to perfection. Aunt Dora was considered the greatest expert, and oversaw the entire process.

As the syrup cooked, a green film was ladled off the top and poured into wooden barrels.

"Make sure you seal those barrels, or you know what happens," Aunt Dora was telling a neighbor.

"What happens?" asked Alfred.

Grandpa Bud chuckled. "The green stuff ferments and changes into alcohol as it ages. Then the cows and pigs get into it. Since we have an open range here, the neighbor cows and pigs also get into it and get drunk. Then they all get hang-overs and headaches and bellow for days."

"That would be fun," said Prent. "I can't wait to see a drunk pig."

☙❧

Fall came and the hot summer sun was forgotten when the children woke to the chilly air. They had to get up when it was even darker and do their chores. The ground was cold, and they appreciated their shoes. Even if they were not new at least they kept their feet warm. They heard stories from others about the cold winters up north with snow. Some of the aunts and uncles had seen snow and talked about how pretty it was. But snow was also cold and everyone needed to wear thick coats and scarves and mittens. "Glad I don't have to buy all 'o that," Papa said.

"Hold your racket," Papa told the kids as they came running out of the woods and into the yard one day. He was standing holding his .22 rifle and looking toward the sky. The kids stopped their play and looked up too.

They saw a hawk circling in the air and slowly descend into one of the tall pines where he landed. The hawk had seen something moving on the ground, and was perched watching steadily for his prey. Little did the hawk know, he was being watched too. Papa's rifle was aimed.

"Bang," the sound of the rifle exploded through the air. The kids gasped.

Then they saw the hawk tumble off the high branch and heard the smaller branches breaking as he fell. They ran yelling to where he lay at the foot of the pine tree. Kenneth jumped up and down with excitement as he tugged to drag the dead bird.

"Mighty tough eatin'," Papa told Mama when she came out to see what was causing the commotion. "Just aimed a foot higher than the bird," Papa explained when people asked him how he had shot a hawk off a tall pine 200 feet away.

Christmas morning, 1935 was a cold windy day. There was no Christmas tree this year. "Don't need a fool tree in the house, when we've got them all over the place all year round. Besides, we aren't wasting berries and corn fixing up a tree," declared Papa.

But Mama had made a wreath out of branches, and decorated it with pine cones. There were candles too, but she didn't light them. The candles needed to be saved for when they were needed.

And the children each got an apple and an orange. "Not much," Papa grumbled, "but ya'all should be thankful for it."

None of them knew what their parents had to live without in order to buy the fruit. Mama had tears in her eyes though, and Alfred knew she wanted to give them more.

Even when he was younger he remembered getting presents. Socks, a little candy, a toy Papa had whittled. That might seem meager to some, but it was a lot to them. But now even those few items were luxuries they couldn't possibly afford.

Papa had gone hunting for a turkey or goose for Christmas dinner, but didn't find one. But they went ahead and splurged and ate one of the egg-laying chickens. Mama made up the bird and all the fixin's she could. It was a wonder how she could do so much when the cupboards were getting bare.

༺༻

The winter got colder. "Least we won't freeze," said Papa as Alfred carried in an armful of wood.

"Too bad we couldn't eat the trees," Alfred thought. "It's about the only thing there is plenty of." Yes, they had plenty of wood for the cook stove, but that didn't solve all of their problems. The cook stove got so hot, that the person cooking in the kitchen would put up a sweat, while those in the next room were shivering with the chilled air. The children would stand at the perfect distance to take advantage of the stove. Even then, the front of them was hot, while their backs were cold.

The weeks of winter continued to pass, and the shelves became emptier and emptier. The chickens weren't laying as much either. Or else there were more chicken snakes helping themselves to the eggs.

The children became hungrier. Many nights Alfred tossed and turned wishing the ache in his belly wasn't there. In the coldest weather, they would pick icicles and eat them, hoping it would ease their hunger.

There was always warm milk. Alfred liked going over to Grandpa Bud's and milking the goats. Best of all, he liked milking Nancy. He would pet and talk to her before getting ready for school each morning.

The porridge got thinner. The slices of bread were thinner. "You're getting thinner too," Miss Annie said to Mama.

That wasn't good; Mama getting thinner. She was expecting a new baby come spring. Papa skipped his meals to try and get Mama to eat more. She just gave it to the children.

One day Mama woke up with a fever and a cough. "It's a goin' around," Miss Annie said. "She'll be a coughing for three or four days and then be herself again."

Mama did cough all that week. But she kept working. She helped with the animals, and continued working in the garden. She had to clean and cook. But it was getting harder to cook, with less and less food available.

One day the kids came home from school and smelled the most delicious smell. Their mouths watered and they hurried through their chores. They hadn't had meat in weeks and wondered what miracle had allowed Mama or Papa to barter for some meat. Oh could Mama cook: meat, and green beans with onions and seasonings, and small pieces of cornbread dipped in gravy. Never had a meal tasted better.

The next morning Alfred rose early as usual to milk Nancy before doing his chores. Nancy wasn't there. She wasn't in the yard, or in the shed. He couldn't find her anywhere.

Nancy? Gone?

The dinner last night – where had it come from? "No, it can't be," Alfred cried. He sat down on the ground clutching his head between his hands. "I don't care if I starve," he sobbed. "I'll never, ever, ever eat goat meat again."

CHAPTER THREE

Mama

It was a chilly March morning, still dark as the sun struggled to come up.

Alfred woke with a start. "School today," he thought as he scrambled out of the bed he shared with Prentice. "I wonder why Mama didn't call us."

From the kitchen he could hear his mother moving around. Quickly, he pulled on his clothes and started for the door. There were always chores to be done before he could eat breakfast and begin the hike to school.

Mama was in the kitchen, struggling to start the fire in the stove. She was bent over with one of her "coughing fits." "Coughing fits" is what Papa called it when Mama coughed so hard she could barely breathe.

"Do you need help Mama?" her son asked.

She nodded yes, her hand on her big belly. Alfred had heard Miss Annie saying Mama would have a baby before the school year was done. For some reason, the grown-ups didn't talk much to the children about babies.

"Alfred, can you.....would you....make sure," Mama was struggling to continue talking, "make sure you....get them to school?" She indicated with her head the rooms where the other kids were sleeping.

Mama was too sick to get the kids up for school. She did not have breakfast made as she usually did. She could not start the kitchen fire.

"Yes, Mama, I'll get them to school," he answered. She said nothing, but doubled over breathing hard. She looked into his eyes before he turned towards the bedroom to call his brother and sister. Her eyes were sad – and worried.

Into the back room, he slipped. "Prent," he shook his brother, "get up." Prentice opened his eyes, and with a moan, pushed back the covers and crept unenthusiastically out. Then Alfred crossed the hallway to the girls' room and called in a loud whisper, "Up, Velma. Mama is sick and needs help before we get off to school today."

In an instant, Velma was up, and crossing the room. She was careful not to wake the smaller sister as she whispered back, "Is Mama still coughing?"

Another coughing spell from the kitchen answered her question. Alfred did not need to reply.

As Velma hurried to the kitchen to help her mother, the two boys headed outside to feed the animals and water the garden. Stale corn bread and cold water from the well had to suffice for breakfast, and were quickly wolfed down by the three kids before they grabbed their school books and started for the door.

Just then, Father came in. "Velma," he grumbled, "ya ain't going to school today. Can't you see your mama needs help here?" Velma meekly put her books down.

"But Father,' responded the older son bravely, who had long ago learned not to cross his father, "Mama wants Velma to go to school."

"Not today I said," Father growled in a rising tone.

Alfred and Velma exchanged looks before she turned and walked silently into the kitchen. Prentice followed Alfred to the door keeping his eyes on the floor.

"You two boys go on off to the school house", continued their Father in a gentler voice. "But we really need Velma here today. I expect Mama might have her little 'un before the day's done."

Two wide pairs of eyes stared at him. The new baby... today?

"Little sooner than we thought," Papa murmured. Their father's voice sounded concerned.

"Now get yourselves off before you're late," he added quickly. "It won't hurt Velma none to miss a day or two of school. She'll be going with ya'all to school again shortly."

But Papa was wrong.

Leaving Velma to help at home, Alfred and Prentice started down the road towards school. Their school house was actually a log cabin. Alfred had heard about the larger schools in some of the bigger towns and cities. Some schools actually had a different classroom for every grade! But he and his parents and grandparents had gone to a one room schoolhouse. He liked school, and he enjoyed the daily walk with Velma and Prentice.

Papa wasn't too kcen on education. Once the brothers over heard their parents arguing whether Alfred had learned enough in school. "I didn't need all that book learnin'," Papa had said. "He ain't gonna need it either. He already can read and write. More'n that is nonsense. Certainly don't help a man put food on the table."

But Mama wanted the kids to go to school. "Best for 'em to learn what they need while they can," she had said.

Today the boys arrived at the school late; and didn't make it into their seats until after the bell rang. Their teacher raised her eyebrows when she saw them come in. Usually it was no small matter when a pupil arrived after the bell. Alfred knew Miss Parker noticed Velma was missing and was wondering why he and Prent were late – a rare occurrence for the usually prompt siblings. But she said nothing. "Likely she'll ask me later," Alfred concluded.

The school day passed as usual. During geography Miss Parker called on Alfred to answer a question about the map at the front. She looked at him quizzically as he fumbled an answer. Most of the time he paid careful attention to the lessons, but today his mind kept returning to thoughts about the new baby. Had he or she been born yet?

During recess the kids played a noisy game of tag. Alfred didn't feel like playing today so he sat with his back against an old pine tree. Miss Parker approached him quietly. "I noticed Velma didn't come with you and Prentice today," she began.

Alfred squinted against the sunlight as he looked up at his teacher. Miss Parker was a no-nonsense teacher. The towns' people often whispered about her since her cousin Bonnie Parker was a notorious bank robber. Almost two years ago Bonnie and Clyde were killed in an ambush. And just last year a trial in Dallas found twenty members of their families guilty of aiding the couple as they hid from the law. But in spite of the rumors, Alfred was sure, Miss Parker had nothing to do with any of it. She lived away from Dallas, away from the publicity, and committed herself to teaching her pupils.

"Yes, Ma'am," Alfred answered his teacher's comment. "Papa said she's to stay home to help Mama."

"Is your mother ill?" the teacher inquired.

"Been coughing a lot lately. Might be having a baby soon." Alfred added.

"I see," Miss Parker responded. "I'm sure you and Velma are both a big help to your parents. But I hope you'll be able to keep up with your school work as well."

"Yes Ma'am," Alfred answered, as he rose to return to the school room with the other students.

He tried hard to pay attention in the afternoon, but was glad when the dismissal bell rang at the end of school. He and Prent grabbed their lunch pails, waved good-bye to their friends and headed straight home. The two brothers raced each other to their house, and arrived at home breathless.

Velma was at the pump washing dirt off Kent's hands and face when they arrived. She looked up at them and motioned towards the house. "It's a boy," Velma called to her brothers. "It's a boy named Joseph."

Father was sitting on the couch holding the new baby, Joseph. Mary Joy was sitting beside him, enthralled with the new bundle wrapped in blankets. Billy, having already looked at the newcomer once or twice was satisfied that he'd seen enough and was lying on the floor nearby playing. Mama was in her room. "She's sleeping," Papa had said, "so just let her be."

Another name was added to the family Bible: Joseph William Bobbitt, born March 23, 1936. His name was written under the other seven names: Elmer who had died at the age of two; Velma, Alfred, Prentice, Kenneth, Mary Joy, Billy, and now little Joseph.

Later that night, Alfred crept into the room to see his mother. He brought her a drink of water from the well. His mother was lying in bed, nursing the baby. She looked so pale, but smiled when he came in.

"Nice baby you got, Mama," he said.

She started to answer, but was interrupted by coughing. She winced as she held her sides.

"You gonna be okay?" he asked her.

"Just hurts here when I cough," she replied. "Coughed so much it makes my muscles ache." It also seemed to make her very tired.

"We went to school today. At least Prent and I did. Velma had to stay and help with the little ones." Mama nodded. She looked so frail.

The next day Prentice and Alfred went to school without Velma again. And the next day. "She's needed here, 'til your Ma gets stronger," their father stated.

Three days after Joseph arrived, Mama got a fever. She continued to cough. That night, Alfred had trouble sleeping. From his room, he could hear his mother coughing much of the night.

Next morning he almost overslept, and had to hurry through his chores in order to get himself and Prentice off to school on time. Velma handed the boys their lunch pails without smiling. She hadn't slept much either.

The two walked in silence for a while down the path through the woods. It was a somber mood between them, and the usual light step and bright look of the younger brother was heavy.

"Is Mama bad sick?" asked the younger brother.

"Seems to be," Alfred responded.

"How come?"

"Pneumonia," Alfred answered. It had been a spelling word he had missed one time, but he knew how to spell it now. That was pretty much all he knew about it. And that it made Mama cough.

"Where does pneumonia come from?"

"Don't know." There wasn't much else to say. They finished the walk to school in silence, and found their way to their desks before the bell rang.

It was a long day, and neither boy concentrated much on his studies. After the bell of dismissal rang, the two started home together. Once again, they didn't stop to talk with the other boys. Instinctively they both knew it was time to get home.

They found Kenneth in the yard making mud pies, and little Billy stepping in them. Prentice handed Alfred his books to take into the house for him as he went to end the mud pie business before Father would see it. Alfred went in the house alone.

It was unnaturally quiet inside. Velma was sweeping the floor. Joseph was lying in his wooden cradle. Alfred went over and looked down at his baby brother, whose breath was coming in little gasps. "He's not breathing good," Velma said, without looking up.

Alfred put away his books and tried to think what he should do next. From the back room came the sound of his mother's coughing. He decided he should go outside and help Prent with the younger kids. It was better outside. The air was crisp, the sun was shining. But the thought of the gasping breaths of his baby brother stayed with him even outdoors.

There were the usual chores to do before dinner. Then the family ate their meal in silence. Papa said nothing. Even Mary Joy and Billy ceased their usual chatter. Should he study his spelling words or do his arithmetic sums? What did it matter?

The older three siblings herded the younger three to bed that night before crawling under the covers themselves. It was a quiet night. Alfred remembered the sound of the pine trees rustling and the occasional cough coming from his parents' room. He heard Mama calling for Papa to bring her the baby, but was interrupted by another fit of coughing. Oh, how we wished he could make her feel better.

Alfred got up and slipped into the hallway. Papa and Velma were near Joseph's cradle. As Alfred walked softly to their side, he noticed that the baby was shaking. Papa picked him up. Little Joseph gasped one more time and then lay quiet in their father's arms. Velma touched the dark hair and stroked Joseph's tiny hand while looking at his face. Pale and lifeless he lay. Their baby brother was dead.

❦

Up the next day. They were not going to school today, but there were chores. Always there were chores. Mama was not in the kitchen, so Alfred gathered the wood and started the fire for her. It was a job that had always made him feel important.

In the living room Mary Joy and Billy were squabbling over an old wooden block.

Billy lost his grip which sent Mary Joy tumbling backwards, dropping the wood with a clamor. A howl went up from both toddlers. Instantly, a door slammed shut and the dark form of their father strode across the room. He grabbed each child by the upper arm and dragged them both off their feet with a shake.

"You be quiet, you hear me?" he yelled in a tone that all of them heard. "Your Ma is sick and I don't want any of your nonsense. All of you, sit down and no more commotion or I'll beat the living daylights out of you. That goes for every last one of you."

The six children sat on the chairs as they were told. They sat there waiting. "What are we waiting for?" Alfred wondered.

He saw Lela Statton come out of Mama's bedroom. Lela was a good friend of their mother's who lived in one of the sharecropper homes on Grandpa Bud's land. She whispered something to their father before going back into Mama's room.

Other neighbors came and spoke in hushed tones. One of the women wrapped Baby Joseph in a new blanket she brought. The kids tried to hear what they were saying, but no one talked to them. Miss Annie gave the children some biscuits to eat for breakfast. None of the children got off their seats.

Alfred jumped up when he saw the tall frame of their grandfather entering the house. Grandpa Bud always knew what to do. No one noticed him as Alfred followed behind his grandfather. He stood outside the door of the room and listened to the voices.

"Gonna be okay, Esper." He heard the low voice of his grandfather. "These land mix-ups happen ya know. Don't worry none about it. We're gonna drop this law suit and everything is gonna be just fine."

Quickly Alfred returned to his seat before his grandfather left. So Grandpa was going to drop the law suit! That was good news.

He thought Papa and Mama would be very happy about that.

But still the children continued to sit quietly and wait. Sometimes they heard Mama cough, but it was a quieter, raspy cough.

As the door to the bedroom opened, Alfred heard Mama calling in a weak voice, "Bring me Joseph. I need to feed my baby." He looked over at the lifeless bundle still lying in the cradle. Mama didn't know.

The morning hours ticked slowly by, and still the children continued to sit in the chairs lined up along the wall. Then Papa came out and announced in an unusually quiet voice, "Your Ma wants to talk to you. All of you. Come 'long now."

Single file the children walked into their parents' bedroom and crowded around Mama's bed. Her eyes lingered on each of them. "I'm real sick," she struggled to say, "and I don't 'spect I'm gonna make it."

She looked over at the two older boys. "Don't want you boys getting into any trouble, you hear? Stay away from drinking and smoking and bad ways. Want all of ya to turn out nice. Be good to others, and each other. You're gonna have to do for each other now. And stay together. That's important, ya know – ya gotta stick together."

Alfred wanted to speak. He wanted to be brave and tell his mother he would take care of everything, just as he had heard his Grandpa do. But his eyes blurred with tears and he couldn't find his voice. All he could do was nod his head.

Velma reached for her mother's hand. "Mama, I love you," she sobbed. Mama squeezed her hand – how weak she was. She smiled at all of them. Then she closed her eyes, still smiling, and fell asleep again.

She never woke up.

After Mama fell asleep, their father jerked his thumb towards the next room. The children went back and took their seats – lined up against the wall from oldest to youngest. Alfred felt numb all over. He saw Prentice looking at him and Velma, waiting for an answer to his questions. But none of them said anything.

Papa walked out of the bedroom. "She's gone now," he muttered to Lela and Miss Annie in a gruff voice.

Next to him, Alfred heard Velma start to sob quietly. Lela walked over and put her arm around Velma's shoulder. She had tears too.

"None of that," Papa barked loudly. "Got too much to do for that nonsense. Ya'all just sit and keep quiet."

Velma wiped her tears and sat up straight. All the children remained silent and still.

More neighbors came. A few men built a pinewood box for both Mama and the baby from some pinewood planks Grandpa Bud brought over. "A casket" Alfred heard one of the neighbors call it.

They put Mama in the casket. The neighbor ladies did their best fixing Mama's hair and her old, patched dress. It was her only dress. The baby was nestled in the crook of Mama's right arm.

"They'll always be together," said Lela. "She'd have liked it that a way."

The next day was cold and rainy. The sun refused to shine. A car came to get the casket and drive it the short distance to the family cemetery – the same cemetery they had all worked to fix up just a few months before. That had been a hot, sunny, happy time. The kids rode with their father in the old wagon.

Someone had dug a deep hole in the soil, and the casket was carried to it. Velma clasped the hands of Mary Joy and Billy on either side of her. Prentice and Alfred kept Kenneth between them. Uncertain of what to expect, they joined the small knot of people gathered around the hole in the earth.

The preacher was there, and started to talk in a quiet voice. Heads nodded, sympathetic glances were directed at the children. Most of the adults in the somber group had suffered the loss of a loved one at least once. For some, the hope of heaven was a reality. For others, the thought was too distant to bring comfort.

Alfred wondered why his mother had died? How could someone who had lived only a few days before really be gone? Who would be there for them when they came home from school? Who was going to cook for them and watch over the little ones?

As adults in the crowd reflected on the questions of life and death one more time, the six children struggled with them for the first time. Alfred glanced at Velma; she had a distant, wild look in her eyes. Prentice seemed confused, as if waiting for an answer no one would give him. The younger children looked scared. Alfred felt the tears forming in his eyes again, but quickly brushed them away.

The preacher's voice stopped. It was quiet. Rain was dripping off the trees. A bird or two chirped somewhere high over head. The wind whistled in the pines. A few men in the crowd stirred and moved to the casket.

Slowly, the casket was lowered into the hole. "No, no" Alfred cried inside. "Don't put Mama in that hole." The casket reached the bottom. Dirt was shoveled on top and the hole was gone.

So was Mama.

CHAPTER FOUR

Hard Times A' Getting Worse

Velma never went back to school again. Alfred and Prent trekked through the pine woods on their way to school without her. The boys no longer raced or played. They often talked less too.

"How come Velma don't come with us no more?" Prent asked one day.

"Papa says she's needed at home," Alfred replied.

As much as it bothered Alfred that his sister wasn't going to school, he could not argue that Velma's help wasn't needed to run the household. With four growing boys and a little sister there was plenty of work for her to do.

But the oldest sister wasn't doing it all by herself, Alfred noted. Little Mary Joy had been recruited into the household chores. At the age of four she made beds, washed dishes, and fed the chickens.

Velma, of course, inherited the more difficult chores that Mama had done. Three meals a day had to be made from scratch. Velma quickly learned where the term "from scratch" came from. She would get up before dawn to try and get eggs from the chicken coop before the snakes beat her to them. She worked in the fields. She tended Mama's garden and canned the fruits and vegetables she pulled out of the dry soil.

A few weeks after the funeral, Alfred was on his bed doing his homework when he heard the squeaking of the front gate. He jumped up happily. The sound of the gate opening and closing often made his heart beat excitedly before he even knew why. But then he always remembered. "It's not Mama coming home after all," he'd realize. That experience repeated itself many times, and every time he remembered, his heart ached.

But tonight, he heard voices in the kitchen. It was one of Mama's brothers and a sister. The conversation was getting loud and angry.

"Think about the children, will you," their aunt was saying. "How are you going to take care of them yourself? Why, you could barely take care of them when Esper was alive."

"And I'll just thank ya for keepin' your blasted opinions to yourselves," stormed Papa. "I don't need nosy relations comin' in and decidin' what's best for my kids."

"Well, who *is* going to decide what is best for the kids?" their aunt retorted.

"And you can just show yourselves the door and don't ever come back," their father's voice bellowed.

Alfred heard the door slam, and a few moments later the sound of a car pulling away.

When his aunt and uncle had left, Alfred slipped cautiously into the kitchen. Papa continued muttering, partially to Alfred, and partially to no one at all.

"Oh sure, your mother's family comes here all high and mighty. 'I'll take Velma' says one. 'We'll take the two older boys says another.' And who's gonna do for the little ones, that's what I'd like to know?" his father ranted.

"Naw, they're just looking for their own farm hands, that's what they's doing," Papa continued. "Notice no one is asking to take the young 'uns, do you? What about little Billy, who is hardly able to talk an' all. 'Put the little ones in an orphanage' they says. Over my dead body!"

And with that, Papa left the house, letting the kitchen door slam shut.

"Papa knows," thought Alfred. "He knows that Mama wants us all to stay together and to go to school."

Their father's tirade had its consequences. The children never saw their mother's relatives again.

A few weeks later as the two oldest sons were crossing the yard on their way to school in the morning, their father hailed them back to the front door.

"Gotta job for you two," he announced. "A neighbor farm is looking for a couple of hands to work helping to place fence posts. You two will be working there the next few weeks."

"But Mama wanted us to go to school," Alfred protested.

"That's nonsense." Their father declared. "School isn't gonna put food on the table. They're paying hands 25 cents a day. That'd be 50 cents a day for the two of you together."

"Besides," he continued," you've had more'n enough studies already. When I was in third grade, I realized I'd had all I needed of that hog wash. Jumped out the window right in the middle of class, I did. And never went back. Never needed to, either. Too much school work will make sissies out of you."

"Mama wasn't a sissy," thought Alfred as his heart sank, "and she wanted us to go to school." However, he also knew Mama wouldn't want the family to go hungry either. Twenty-five cents a day! In two weeks that would be six dollars that he and Prent would earn. That would buy a lot of beans to ease their hunger pains.

So the two boys headed off to work as farm hands. They would work one week here, two weeks there. In between they went to the one room school house. But as time went on, they were seen at their desks less often. Finally, the school dropped them from the rolls due to lack of attendance.

"We'll be going back again soon," Alfred consoled himself and his siblings, "just as soon as we can sell enough crops to make enough money."

Father never objected if his kids wanted to study at home. Whenever he could, Alfred stayed up late to study his books. But many times, he was too tired from the hard day's work, and fell asleep as soon as the evening chores were done.

At the general store two old gentlemen were enjoying their tobacco and the fresh morning air. They noticed a tall figure turning the corner, and they waved in return to his wave as he strode by. He passed them and turned into the local bank.

"Hey, that's Alfronzie Bobbitt. Now what da ya suppose he's a going into the bank for," asked the one.

"Same as everyone else nowadays, likely," came the answer. "Probably needing a loan to plant crops this year."

"Mighty shame about the missus," said the first. "With all them little 'uns to feed and all."

The old gentlemen were right. It was Papa and he had gone to the bank to get a loan so he could plant crops that spring. Nothing was left from the proceeds of last year's harvest. The only problem was that the bank wanted collateral for the loan. Collateral are things of value that a borrower owns. If a borrower is unable to repay his loan, the collateral would belong to the bank.

What could Papa use as collateral? Some of the farmers put their land up for collateral. Many family farms were lost during the Depression when the farmer couldn't pay back the bank.

But Alfronzo Bobbitt had more problems than some of the other farmers. He claimed that the land he farmed was his. But his father, Grandpa Bud, also claimed to own that land. The banks would not accept that land as collateral since there was a lawsuit over who owned it.

Alfred was very surprised and disappointed that Grandpa Bud had not kept his promise he made when Mama was sick. He had not dropped the law suit over the homestead land. That surprised many people, especially Alfred, because Grandpa Bud was known as a man of his word. And what promise would be more binding than one made to a dying kin?

"It's Miss Annie that's put him up to keeping that lawsuit going," one of the old gentlemen claimed. "She's a step-mother to Old Bud's kids. Doesn't take too kindly to Alfonzie or some o' the others, I hear."

Alfronzo came strolling out the bank and again gave a wave of acknowledgement to the town gossips. He had indeed got cold cash in his pocket from a bank loan. But since the lawsuit was still pending, he was not able to put the land up as collateral. All he had was his farm tools and horse and two mules. But at least he now had some money to plant crops.

The cash in Alfronzo's pocket was taken to the feed store and exchanged for seeds and a few other farm implements. Then the precious seeds were planted into the soil that spring of 1936.

Velma, Alfred, Prentice, Kenneth, Mary Joy, and even little Billy toiled with their father in the fields. It was a dry summer. The water in Bobbitt Creek got lower and lower. Some of the chickens and other small animals died. It was always hot, and sticky and uncomfortable in the blazing heat. The farmers all waited for the rain to come, at first patiently, then anxiously.

But the rain never came. The plants were burnt in the fiery, Texas sun. Day by day, their hopes withered with the crops.

One afternoon as Alfred crossed the woods from Grandpa Bud's house, he noticed a truck stopped in front of his house. An armed sheriff was there. Two men were leading the horse and mules into the truck. He saw the tools that Papa had worked so hard to buy were already in the back of the vehicle.

As the truck pulled away, Prentice held onto Kenneth who was tugging to get away. "No, no," little Kenny was shouting, "you can't take our animals from us!"

"How are we going to farm without our animals and tools?" Alfred wondered, dumbstruck by what he had just witnessed. He saw his father stomp off into the woods, his fists clinched.

There is a great irony about the Great Depression, this period when Alfred grew up. An irony is the opposite of what you might expect. Year after year crops failed, and farmers lost everything. The soil stubbornly refused to yield the crops that everyone so badly needed.

But instead of crops, that stubborn soil produced something else: a generation of equally stubborn, hard workers. They didn't think others owed them a job – because jobs were scarce. They made work themselves. If one could earn ten cents an hour whittling sticks or making something with their hands, they would stay up late an extra three hours doing it. And be glad for it too. If they could build a fence, they would get up early in the morning to build one for an older neighbor in exchange for a few eggs. If you could teach or clean or fold or sew or lift heavy things or pack light things you did it in exchange for some milk or a used pair of shoes.

They pinched pennies and made what little they had last as long as it could. They helped each other too. These hard working children never imagined that one day they would become one of the wealthiest generations that ever lived. But they didn't understand that then. The children of the Depression only hoped to get a little food for one more day.

One day as Alfred was chopping wood for winter, he heard a carriage pull up in front of his house. He went around the corner to see who the visitor might be. To his surprise, his father and an unknown woman left the carriage and went into the house.

"This is your new ma," Papa was saying to the kids when Alfred came in. The children stared at her. She didn't look anything like their Mama, Alfred thought. She wasn't tall and dark. Her hair and skin seemed pale, her eyes less friendly. The kids weren't sure they liked the new mama; and she wasn't sure she liked them.

Bertha was the name of their father's new wife. Sometimes Papa and Bertha would argue. Papa punished his children if they argued with each other, but it didn't seem to stop the two adults from arguing. None of the kids liked it when their father and step-mother shouted at each other.

But there was something worse than listening to Bertha arguing with their father.

"This water isn't hot enough; you won't get any dishes clean like that," Alfred heard Bertha complaining to Velma as he was reading one evening.

"You're filling the jars too full," Bertha snapped as Velma was canning tomatoes.

It made Alfred angry to hear his sister being criticized by their step-mother. "Velma," Alfred thought, "does more work around here than she does."

It was hard for Velma to lose the mother she loved. It was difficult to work hard all the time and never have time to talk with friends. It was hard to be young and have to raise three small children under the age of five. Then having an insensitive step-mother move in and criticize her was unbearable.

So Velma left home. She was still quite young, but she got married two years after Mama died. She married Willis who was a cattle farmer.

Alfred thought Willis was a good man, but he had misgivings about his sister leaving.

"Are you sure you want to do this," he inquired when he and Velma were alone. "I mean, do you really want to marry Willis."

"Yes, yes, I do," Velma assured him. "He's been kind to me."

"But, I don't want you to leave," her brother protested.

"I won't be far away, Alfred," his sister reminded him. "And I want you to bring the little ones over to visit. Willis says it okay – he wants them to come. But don't bring..." she tilted her head to the next room where her step-mother was.

Alfred nodded his agreement. "I'll bring the kids over. I promise."

Things did not get better with Papa and his new wife. Sometimes Bertha left. She might be gone for months at a time and they didn't know where she went.

"I don't care she's gone," Alfred grumbled to Prent one day as they were working in the fields. Papa wasn't around to overhear.

"Me neither," retorted Prentice. "It'll suit me just fine if she stays away for good."

But she did come back. One day Bertha came back with some of her own kin that she had been staying with. She took some of the food that Papa and the kids had grown on their farm and gave it to her relatives. Alfred was angry whenever she took their food.

Finally, Papa divorced her. Then, to Alfred's dismay, he remarried Bertha again. But the arguments continued. Eventually, their step-mother disappeared for the last time and never returned.

Velma was gone. The new wife was gone. Little Mary Joy had to take over all the cleaning and cooking.

Early one morning as Alfred, Prentice and Kenneth were talking in the bedroom, they heard Papa shouting and Mary Joy crying. The boys rushed to see what was wrong.

"No, Papa, I'm sorry. No, I won't. Stop, please, stop." Mary Joy was pleading. They found Papa in the kitchen with one of his shirts twisted several times into a makeshift belt, and he was whipping Mary Joy with it. Alfred wanted to protest, but he was afraid of his father's temper.

"Don't ever do that again!" their father shouted at the little girl lying on the kitchen floor as he stormed out of the house. Alfred stared at the welts starting to form on his little sister's legs.

She had ironed the shirt wrong.

Papa didn't want to be a bad man. He was brave, but he was scared. Everything had been going bad for years. Hadn't he worked hard and tried everything? Since the Depression had started he had owned a store that failed, he had been a sharecropper, he had bought a farm, had worked as a carpenter, a mechanic, a bridge builder, and obtained a "wagoning" license to take children to school in his own wagon. He had tried to keep his family together and to find a new mama for the kids.

But there was even more bad news. The homestead case had gone to court. The judge listened to both sides. He heard how Grandfather Bud had been living on the homestead for years, and was farming both halves: the half owned by himself and the half owned by their grandmother who was now dead for eighteen years. Because he was a homesteader, he should be allowed to keep both halves until he died and continue farming them, Grandpa Bud argued. Bud explained that his son Alfronzo had come to live on the land as sharecroppers, but after a few years refused to give him half of the crops any more.

The judge also heard Papa's side of the story. He heard that when Alfronzo's mother died, her half of the estate belonged to her nine children. Alfronzo told how he and

Esper worked hard and saved every penny they could, and how after the first two years of working the homestead they had bought their own seeds, animals, and farm tools. If they were sharecroppers, he debated, then the land owner was supposed to supply those; but he had bought them himself.

Alfonzo showed the judge the deeds. He had bought 68 acres of the land from some of his brothers and sisters for $1 an acre, and they had agreed to sell it to him because that was the price of land in San Augustine County at that time. Alfronzo and his kids were not sharecroppers, because they had bought the land from the rightful heirs, and they bought their own farm supplies.

In the end, the judge agreed with Grandpa Bud. He ruled that Bud was a homesteader and had the right to run the entire estate until his death, even if his wife had already died. Alfonzo and the children were evicted from the farm house.

Now they had no home.

What do you do when everything has gone wrong for a long time? Do you give up? Not when you have young children depending on you and you want to do your best for them. Not when you have a good head and strong hands that are ready to work. Papa was determined to find a way to provide for his family.

Alfred and Prentice were uncertain of the future. They helped their father carry their possessions to the wagon. Where would they go now?

Alfred looked at the house, the only home he really remembered. His eyes lingered on his mother's garden, the shed where he had milked Nancy, the creaking gate that always made him hope Mama was coming home. He looked at the path leading to his grandfather's house and the man who meant so much to him.

"The trees, the trees! It's the pines!" he heard his father exclaim. He turned to look at his father who was staring up at the top of the pine trees. Had their father gone crazy?

"Not beans and peas and cotton," their father uttered. "The real crop here is the pine trees!"

Papa was right! The farm crops had failed, but there was yet another crop growing out of that old Texas soil: the pine trees. They were tall and strong and had withstood the fiery drought. The yellow pines grew fast in that soil and could be replaced.

So Papa decided to become a logger.

"They're clearing timber only a few miles from here," Papa said as their wagon headed down FM 1751, pulled by a team of mules borrowed from Grandpa Bud. "You two boys can help," he said to Alfred and Prentice. "We'll just live out in the woods 'til we get a little more money saved," he added.

"We're gonna live in the woods?" Alfred asked.

"Why not?" their father responded. Gotta live somewhere. I got some canvas, and can make a tent."

"We're gonna live in a tent?"

"Ya'all wanna sleep under the sky, or under a tent?" their father answered.

Turning off of the Sabinetown Road, the wagon headed into a thickly wooded area. They stopped and Papa unhitched the mules. He left the kids and the wagon, and headed off by himself with one of the mules.

These woods were similar to those on the Bobbitt Homestead, but the trees were more crowded together. Alfred took a deep breath. The same pine fragrance surrounded him. Kenneth and Billy started throwing pine cones and chasing each other.

"This might not be so bad after all," Prentice said. "Kind a like camping."

"And how am I supposed to wash the dishes?" Mary Joy asked.

When Papa came back, everything was arranged. "We're gonna be hauling logs to the J.B. King Sawmill," he announced. They got a contract with the Temple Lumber Company in Pineland."

The children helped move all their possessions into the one room tent. The tent was about 30 feet by 30 feet with a wooden floor. Short wooden walls about three feet high came from the floor to a height a little above Alfred's knees. The canvas roof was held up by a long pole in the center of the tent and tied to the wood at the four corners.

"Mighty good thing we live here in Texas, and not up north in one of them states that gets snow," he told his children.

The first night was the hardest. There were only four beds, so the boys had to share. Alfred lay in the bed he shared with Prentice and listened to his father's snoring. The sound of a nearby owl hooting made him sit up with fright.

"What was that?" Kenneth asked.

"Just an old owl," Alfred answered, trying to keep his voice from shaking. He lay back down.

"Hey, Alfred?" Prentice whispered.

"Yes."

"Are there bears in these woods?"

"Naw. Never seen a bear in these woods. Bears are up further north."

There was a moment of silence.

"Alfred?" asked another voice.

"What Kenneth?"

"Are there any tigers in these woods?"

"No tigers either," the older brother answered. "They live in Africa and couldn't get to Texas if they wanted to."

"Alfred?"

"What is it, Billy?"

"Are there any dragons in the woods?"

"No, Billy, there aren't any dragons. None in Texas or any place else."

"But there are scorpions, tarantulas, and rattlesnakes," Alfred thought to himself. He didn't tell them what he was thinking.

Early the next morning, Alfred woke when the first beams of light crept into the tent. Their father was already up.

"Come on," he said. "You're gonna do some logging today."

Mary Joy and Billy stayed behind at the tent. Alfred, Prentice, and Kenneth went with their father.

"What's Kenneth gonna do?" asked Alfred.

"He's good with animals. He can lead the mules," Papa answered. Little Kenny straightened up, looking at his older brothers with pride.

"Our father certainly is hard working," Alfred told Mary Joy one evening, several weeks after they moved into the tent. "He works harder than any other logger in all of Texas."

"Works us hard too," Prentice added.

"Right about that," agreed Billy, who had joined his brothers in the logging after the first few days.

Their father certainly was industrious. His sons noticed it, and others did too. Once again, Papa saved his hard earned wages, and bought himself his own equipment and mules to move the precious timber from the woods to the mills.

They also had a wood burning stove that Mary Joy used for cooking, and a wood burning heater for the cold months. A smoke stack rose from the heater about six feet, then made a 90 degree turn and went out a metal flue in the tent. But, Alfred sadly noted, there was no light to allow him or the others to read.

"Times will get better," Alfred reasoned. "Then we'll be able to study and go to school again."

After six months, the tent was replaced. Their father used wood planks from his logging operation to build six wooden boxes about six by twenty feet. Each box was about the size of a bathroom in modern homes. Alfred and Prentice helped him build the pinewood boxes.

One box room was a kitchen, and another was their living room. Prent and Alfred shared a room; and Billy and Kenneth shared one room. Father and Mary Joy each had their own rooms. The six boxes all had three walls and a floor. The fourth side was open.

Papa put the boxes in two rows, with three on each side and a hallway down the middle. He showed the boys how to build temporary walls with plywood to connect the six different rooms. Then they put pieces of plywood on top of the boxes to make a roof.

This made a portable house for the family. The boxes could be taken apart and moved to an area of woodland they were clearing. Then, when it was time to move again, they would once again take down the walls and the roof and move the boxes that made up their house.

With his sons, Papa had an entire crew to do the logging. Alfred and his three younger brothers became the loggers. Because he didn't have to pay his sons any wages, Papa's logging business was quite successful. Some people in government and in business talked about a possible war in Europe. Ships were built, and military bases were constructed. That meant wood was needed, and someone needed to get the wood to the mills. The Depression was finally ending.

No longer were they up before dawn to feed chickens and milk goats. They were still up early, and Mary Joy always made three large meals a day from her pine box kitchen. Felling trees and moving logs is man's work. Alfred was growing tall and strong. The other boys were strong and growing too. They had to be, to cut the trees, roll the timber, hoist the logs onto the platform, drive the mules, and unload the cargo. Mary Joy was kept busy, feeding the hungry crew with their voracious appetites.

Papa invented an A-Frame device to load the logs onto the platform. "He is unbelievably smart," the mechanic who welded the A-Frame reported to others. "He could devise and build anything he set his mind to."

Papa's new invention used the power take-off on the truck's transmission to spear and load the logs. His invention was far ahead of any other log loading method in East Texas at that time.

There were plenty of logs that needed to be moved, enough jobs for their crew, and – finally – enough food to eat. Once again, Alfred heard Papa humming as he went about his work. The four young boys each did the work of at least one man. It was hard work, but they were proud of it.

But, of course, once the logging business started, none of them could ever go to school again.

CHAPTER FIVE
Coming Home

World War II was over. It was 1949. Far away across the ocean, Europe was recovering from the Great War. Men and women from small towns throughout the United States found themselves in foreign lands. Young people who came from families too poor to travel ended up on the other side of the globe. Even the well-to-do slept in leaky tents or quickly built barracks on military bases.

Alfred Bobbitt from San Augustine County, Texas found himself in Germany on a Friday night in early 1949. He was part of the Berlin Airlift, code named *Operation Vittles.*

When the Soviet Union surrounded the city of Berlin, Germany after the end of the war, President Truman had ordered supplies flown over the blockade. Alfred was one of many airmen who undertook the massive campaign to get supplies to the people of Berlin. More than 13,000 tons of food and fuel a day were dropped from C-54's to the ground below.

After the last C-54 was loaded with supplies and had taken off down the runway, Alfred joined the other military men and women standing in long lines waiting for their pay. At the front of the line, clerks sat with cash boxes. The enlisted person would tell the clerk their name and rank when they finally reached the front. One month's salary was then given in cash.

Alfred was now third in line. A friendly young man, he spent the thirty minutes in line chatting with the other airmen near him. They shared stories about their current mission or their previous assignments during the war. Alfred had been stationed in Panama, Central America as an army soldier during the war. Shortly after getting out of the US Army, he had joined the newly formed United States Air Force.

Finally Alfred was at the front of his line. "Sergeant Alfred Bobbitt" he stated, and the clerk counted one hundred and forty seven dollars of cash into his hand. That was his salary for the month. He took the money and started off towards the barrack that he shared with others in the Air Force.

"Hey, Al," shouted a voice behind him, "do you want to go the bar with us?" It was one of his roommates. Friday night after pay day was usually a time of drinking and partying for many of the single men on the base. With the coming of the war, the Great Depression had ended. Now with more than $100 in their pockets, young men were ready for some form of entertainment.

"No," Alfred replied, "I've got some other things I need to do with my time and money." The others kidded their bunk mate and drove off.

Alfred had his faults, including the occasional hot temper noted in many of the men in his family. However, drinking, gambling, and wasting money were not among them. And, just as he had said, he had other things to do with his money.

When he got to his barrack he took out a sheet of paper and pen. "Dear Mary Joy," he began his letter to his sister.

There was no thought of joining the guys at the bar or losing his money in a poker game. He had younger brothers and a sister still at home. In this particular letter, he broke down how much he was sending her for books and clothing.

After finishing this letter, he addressed and sealed it and decided he would post it the next day. Then, as Alfred lay in bed, he mentally went through the needs of his family back home.

Velma and Willis were doing fine. Even though Velma had left home when she married, the rest of the kids went to her home as often as they could, and she generously cooked delicious meals for them. Velma was quite quick to respond to all letters Alfred sent her.

Prentice was an aircraft engine mechanic in the Army Air Corp. Thankfully, he had not been sent out of the country, though he had served in Alaska and Florida. Before going into the military, Prentice and Alfred had owned a Mobile gas station together. But then Alfred had been drafted, and both brothers ended up in the army.

His father's logging business had ended when regulations against child labor had prevented him from continuing with his sons as his crew. His father had moved back to the Bobbitt Homestead briefly, and then moved to Dallas, Texas.

Kenneth had gone to school off and on as he was able and was working now as a farmer and carpenter. "That boy always liked working the land," thought Alfred. Letters from their sisters hinted that Ken was falling in love with Sue, the daughter of his own mother's friend Lela. Memories of children hoeing, weeding, picking crops and feeding animals returned to him. His family and the children of the other sharecropping families worked hard trying to coax produce from that ground to feed themselves and their livestock. Some, like Kenneth, loved the work.

Mary Joy was now going to high school. Her father wanted her to work and contribute to the family income instead of going to school. But, at Alfred's insistence, Papa accepted money that he sent home so his sister could finish school. Prentice also sent money home to help the family. Mary Joy was planning to go on to a business college which Alfred heartily agreed to. "A practical skill for her," concluded the pragmatic brother, who thought business college was a sound investment for her.

But as he thought about the youngest brother, even in the dark Alfred's face narrowed with concern. "Don't got no use for that confounded book learnin," Bill would say whenever Alfred pushed him regarding his education. He had dropped out of school and nothing would make him go back. He worked as a carpenter's assistant, and had no career ambitions beyond that.

"At least finish high school," the eldest brother coaxed. But the youngest child would not budge.

Alfred recalled how much he himself had wanted to go to school, and how he tried to study when he could. It had seemed like a lost cause.

But maybe it wasn't. After Alfred had been drafted at the age of 18, he and Prent went to school for a few months before he was sent overseas. After three months, the school gave him an honorary diploma, even though he had never gone past fourth grade. All the nights he had diligently studied old school books in dim light were finally rewarded. "Maybe," thought Alfred, "I'll be able to go to college some day. And so will the others back home."

Night after night Alfred thought about his plans and reviewed the needs of his siblings. He did again this night after writing to Mary Joy. He also wrote that he would be coming home in a few months to visit while he was on leave from the Air Force.

In the spring of 1949, the young Sergeant Bobbitt arrived back in Pineland, Texas. It was too early in the morning for anyone to expect a call, so he stopped at a local diner for coffee and breakfast.

He slid into a booth and looked over the menu. Shortly a young waitress in a checkered apron approached the table with a cheerful smile which Alfred politely returned. As he gave his order, her smile froze and she fumbled with her pad. She glanced at him nervously as she poured his coffee. Then she disappeared into the kitchen.

"Surely she has seen a military uniform before," thought the young Bobbitt, who wasn't sure what it was about his presence that had flustered her so much. But those thoughts were interrupted as he heard a familiar laugh and turned around to see Prent walking towards him. Prentice was finishing his term in the army and returning home to stay. His brother slid into the booth and the two started talking at once.

The befuddled waitress returned to the table and almost dropped Alfred's plate on his lap. She looked back and forth between the two men. "I, I thought you were him," she stammered, "and couldn't figure out why you were acting different. Plus," she added, "you are wearing the wrong uniform."

Prentice, it turned out, had sat at that same booth almost every morning that week. The two look-alike brothers laughed at the mix up. It was neither the first time nor the last that it would happen.

The two brothers talked about the war, military life, and the changes in their lives. And then they talked about the family.

"Velma tells me Mary Joy is doing well in high school and plans to go on to college," remarked Prentice.

"So I gathered from both of their letters," replied Alfred, "and I'm glad to hear it. But it is Billy I really worry about," he continued. "I have told him time and again he needs to go to school and prepare for a job, but he doesn't listen. Never did listen to any sense, and never will," Alfred finished with a disapproving shake of his head.

"Come on, give the kid a break, will you Alfred," the younger brother responded. "Do you have any idea how other kids picked on him? And with his cleft palate no one understood what he said when the teacher called on him. It was harder for him than you may realize."

"He should still try to better himself anyway. Problem with teenagers is they think they know everything. And he is too stubborn and headstrong to listen to anyone else."

Prent just answered with a raised eyebrow. The older brother realized Prent thought *he* was the one who was stubborn and headstrong.

"Well, whatever you think of his schooling," Prent continued, "the kid has turned out to be a pretty good carpenter. You oughta take a look at some of his work."

"I'll do that. Not surprised he can build though," continued Alfred. "He worked with our father first as a logger in these woods; then building homes with him in Dallas. Both our father and grandfather were pretty good with a hammer."

"And just about any other tool imaginable," added Prentice.

"True. But you know, the one thing I never could quite understand is why Grandpa Bud had us evicted from our own home. And he was always so good to us, too," Alfred reflected.

"Kind of strange," Prentice agreed. "But I've been talking to Aunt Dora and Aunt Lou some since I got back. They explained it from a different perspective."

"How's that?"

"Well, here's how I see it. Remember when you and I owned the gas station together before we went in the army? Just think if we had a relative who needed a job, so we hired him to work in our store in order to help him out a bit. At first he's happy he's got a job. Then he decides he'd rather do things his own way. Next thing you know he puts a few of his own groceries on the shelf, and states that he can now keep all the money the customers pay when they buy things. That's basically what our father did when he went to live on the farm as a sharecropper, but then later refused to turn over the crops to Grandpa."

"That makes sense. Grandpa Bud was getting too old to do all the work himself, but needed the four sharecroppers to pay their half so he could keep the farm going."Alfred agreed. "When our father didn't turn over his half of the crops, it was taking money not only from our grandfather but from his other children who would inherit the land when he died."

"But on the other hand, we would have starved if he had paid them," mused Prentice.

"We just about starved anyway. In the end, it was probably a good thing we were evicted."

"Sure didn't seem like that then. But now, some of our relatives are complaining that we stole land from them."

"What?" asked Alfred in surprise. "What relatives? How can anyone say we stole land when we were evicted from it?"

"Well," answered Prent slowly. "Remember you told me that our father bought land from our aunts and uncles when we were children?"

"Yes, he did. That was one of the reasons he felt he wasn't a sharecropper."

"So, now some are saying that the amount he paid during the Depression wasn't enough. He paid the amount it was worth back then, which was only $1 an acre. But it's worth more now."

"Well, they took his money and signed over the deed back when $1 was hard to earn and even harder to save," argued the older brother.

"Look, I'm not arguing with you," Prent replied. "I'm only telling you what some of our relatives have said. Maybe you should discuss it with Velma since she's been living in Pineland for all these years."

"I will. In fact, I was planning on seeing Velma this morning."

"Velma isn't going to be home until tonight; she went with Willis to see about some new heifers. I told our cousin Ray I would meet him for fishing this morning. Do you want to come with us?"

"Not today," Alfred answered. "I guess I'll head over towards the homestead and see how Kenneth's farming is going. Maybe I'll have lunch with him."

❦

The brothers parted from each other for the morning and went their separate ways. Alfred headed over towards Farm Market 1751 but didn't see any sign of Kenneth. He started to walk through the woods, and the scent of pine needles and the crunching sound under his feet stirred up old memories. Without even noticing it, he was heading towards his grandfather's homestead.

The house was empty. Abandoned. His grandfather had died four years before. Alfred had returned home as soon as he had heard of his grandfather's death, but missed the funeral by two hours. Now, Miss Annie was also gone and the homestead deserted.

"He was my best friend," the somber young man reflected. The door was ajar, and Alfred walked in. He sat down on the hearth where he had sat on his Grandpa Bud's lap and listened to stories so long ago. "My earliest memories, he thought. He heard the sound of small, wild animals shuffling through the pine needles in the yard, and thought of the goats. He thought of Nancy, and milking her and playing with her.

In the corner, the broken mirror of an equally dilapidated set of dressers stood. Alfred caught a reflection of himself in uniform in the mirror. "I think Grandpa would be proud of me," he thought.

The stillness made his heart ache. He got up and started down the path away from Grandpa Bud's homestead. So familiar and comforting are the sights and sounds of home to the returned soldier. But the heart has changed. He was restless and wanted to walk. And think.

As a young boy at his grandfather's lap, he had heard stories of battles long ago. There were stories about cowboys and Indians; Civil War stories of the Confederates and the Yankees. But he was no longer a little boy. He had seen the devastation of war. He had struggled with the great lesson those on both sides of most wars had trouble understanding – that one group of people cannot demand their rights while denying them to others. How many more wars would the world see before everyone would understand that?

Alfred thought of the part he had played in the Berlin Airlift that dropped food to the starving people in Germany. He smiled when he remembered the controversy of dropping candy bars. At first the men who did it were reprimanded by their superiors. But then the newspapers carried the story to the rest of the world. It was so popular with the public that they were allowed to continue sending candy from parachutes to the ground below.

"What would it have been like for me and my brothers and sisters if food and candy bars had dropped from the sky when we were so hungry?" he wondered. He looked up at the tall, familiar pine trees and tried to imagine bundles of food dropping.

No, there had been no falling food in those days. They had chopped and plowed and planted and picked to get what meager meals they did have. The older children provided for the younger ones; and the younger ones helped the older ones. Meal by meal, day after day, the years had passed.

And they had survived. The oldest and youngest in his family had died in infancy, but the other six plodded through the years of the Depression to become young adults in a new and different era.

Their father had been industrious and worked hard to get food and the most basic necessities. "But it takes more than just food to take care of a family," Alfred reflected.

His mother had known that. She had wanted more for her children than she had been able to provide. But she never stopped hoping.

His wandering steps took him to the family cemetery, still a small fenced in plot. He noticed a few new graves – a second cousin; an older aunt. There was Grandpa Bud's tombstone. He was buried next to his first wife, Alfred's real grandmother. Miss Annie, who died just two years ago, was buried at his grandfather's feet.

"This cemetery is a place of life, not death," his grandfather had told him many years before. "Here is the story of the family you come from."

"My family," Alfred mumbled quietly.

Every tombstone told just a little piece of the story that had been lived. Joy and pain were woven through those stories.

But it was more than just the story of one family. Here was history. The names on these gravestones might not make it into the history books, but these were the people who had lived it. Here were the tradesmen who had built their communities. Here were the farmers who had fed Texas. Here were the soldiers who had fought the battles of their nation. These were the men and women and children who had subdued the land and loved it.

Automatically, his steps carried him to the grave of his mother. The mound was no longer fresh. The flowers were gone. "Thirteen years," thought Alfred. He stood reverently with his hand over his heart, feeling the sun on his back and the crisscross pattern of sun light breaking through the shadows of the pine trees.

But the pain in his chest and the tightness in his throat returned as he thought of that rainy March day thirteen years ago. Six pairs of young eyes had stared in confusion and grief as her casket had been lowered in the grave. Then he had felt so small, but had wanted to be brave.

"I tried to keep my promise, Mama," he whispered. He heard the birds singing overhead and the wind whistling in the tall pine trees.

Epilogue

Augustus Tentamous LaFamous Bobbitt, Jr. (1861-1945) is Grandpa Bud in this story. He was born and died on the Bobbitt Homestead, and was the third generation to farm it. His first wife was Elizabeth Dickerson, and they had 13 children, four of whom died as infants. His second wife was Anna Riley Brown, known as "Miss Annie" to the step-grandchildren. "Bud was a generous man, oftentimes helping relatives and neighbors with food and money and a place to live," is one of many descriptions his grandson wrote in a twelve page mcmoire of his grandfather.

Alfonzo Iza Bobbitt (1899-1955) was the Papa in this story. After the logging business ended in 1943 due to child labor regulations, he moved back to the Bobbitt Homestead for about a year, and then to Dallas, Texas where he was able to get work building homes. However, he loved the homestead, and visited it frequently. After his father died, Alfonzo was given clear title to the 68 acres he had purchased in the early 1930's, in spite of objections from some relatives who had sold it. He was married to a third wife but they were divorced after a number of years. "He was a farmer, carpenter, blacksmith, bridge builder, logger, mechanic and business owner," wrote his son years later. He is buried in the Bobbitt Cemetery next to his first wife and the mother of all his children.

Mary Esper Robbins Bobbitt (1905-1936) was the Mama of the family. Both of Esper's parents were descendants of Thursa Carter, a Choctaw Indian, and Richard Fonville, a white farmer from Alabama. Like her husband, Esper was born and grew up in the pined woods of rural, San Augustine County, in the east part of Texas. She was married right before she turned 16, and worked on the farm much of her life. Alfred described his mother: "She was a hard worker, doing the best she could with what little she sometimes had to do with, tending to a large vegetable garden, canning all kinds of fruits and vegetables, milking cows, working the fields and looking after six children. She loved her family. Esper literally worked herself to death." She was always missed by her children after her early death.

Elmer Bobbitt (1922-1924) was the first child in Alfonzo and Esper's family, but died after choking on a peanut shell while visiting Grandpa Bud and Miss Annie's house the month before Velma was born. She is buried to the left of her mother.

Velma Rachel Bobbitt Morris Sloan. Velma still lives in Pineland, Texas, just a few miles south of the Bobbitt Homestead. After the death of her first husband, Willis, she remarried, and continued raising Angus cattle and working as a secretary. She and Willis adopted two of Billy's children's after his first marriage ended. She is active with her grandchildren, and in the community. She was on the Pineland City Council for over ten years, serving as mayor pro tem in the 1980's. She is an excellent cook, and the fourth generation of Bobbitt children now enjoy the meals from her kitchen.

Alfred Fonzie Bobbitt (1926-2003) After serving in the military for over twenty years, Alfred settled in Bellevue, Nebraska where he started and managed his own insurance agency with the help of his wife and children. Over the years, he continued his education through night school whenever he found time, and finally graduated from Bellevue College at the age of 50. Always an advocate for learning, he encouraged everyone – relatives, neighbors, even strangers - to pursue their education. All four of his kids have degrees in teaching or education. In the last decade of his life, he compiled a family genealogy, from which much of the material in this story was gleaned. He died of a stroke at the age of 76, and is missed by his 12 grandchildren whom he loved dearly.

Alvy Prentice Bobbitt. Prentice lived for a while in Pineland after leaving the military, then settled in his wife's home town in Stockton, Kansas where they raised their six children. He owned and operated Bobbitt Equipment Company which sold and serviced farm equipment. Even the children of Alfred and Prentice would occasionally mix the two of them up. Both families enjoyed their annual Halfway Picnic – midway between Bellevue and Stockton. Even though he is retired, Prent continues to farm and he and his wife, Betty, enjoy having their children, grandchildren, and great-grandchildren near them in Stockton, Kansas.

Kenneth Ray Bobbitt (1930-2004) Kenneth settled in Pineland, Texas and acquired most of the Bobbitt land owned by his father which he and his sons continued to farm and run herds of cattle. In 1950 he married Sue, the daughter of Lela, who was also born on the Bobbitt Homestead. As a child he usually drove teams of mules or horses in the logging business. As an adult he became a carpenter and cabinet maker, but continued to do logging, farming, and tending his herd of cattle. He and two of his sons are buried in the family cemetery. Another son and daughter, and many grandchildren, still live in East Texas. His youngest son continues to raise cattle on the land owned by his great-great-great grandparents.

Mary Joy Bobbitt moved to the Dallas area with her father after the end of his logging business in 1943. She graduated from the Dallas public schools and went to North Texas State University. She worked as a legal secretary for more than 40 years. For a short time she lived with her husband in Langley Field, Virginia before returning to Dallas. For 56 years, she made the five hour trip from Dallas to Pineland to visit her siblings and nephews and nieces whenever she was able. She has also enjoyed her trips to foreign countries. Recently, she settled in Nacogdoches, near Pineland and close to her childhood home.

Billy Ray Bobbitt, Sr. (1934 – 1989) also lived in Dallas and Pineland. His first two children were adopted by his sister, Velma, after his divorce. In a subsequent marriage he raised a son and step son. Apprenticed as a carpenter by his father, Billy became a highly skilled and accomplished carpenter whose work was in much demand in the region. He died of a heart attack at the age of 54 and is buried to the right of his parents.

Joseph William Bobbitt (March 23 to March 27, 1936) was Esper's youngest child who was born right before her death, and was buried nestled in her arm. "He was a beautiful baby," his sister Velma remembers. "Even though he was born early, he was absolutely perfect." When his brothers and sisters became adults, they erected a marble tombstone for their parents, and had "Baby Brother" inscribed in the middle.

The Bobbitt Cemetery is still there on Farm Market Road 1751, just 17 miles south of San Augustine, Texas. A Texas State Historical Marker lists this as one of the earliest remaining sites of white settlers, which began with the burial of Little Alfonzo, the son of Augustus Tentamous LeFamous Bobbitt Sr. (Aug) The graves of many of the people mentioned in this story can be seen there, as well as many others. If you visit the Sunday of the Bobbitt Reunion, you will find their great-great-grandchildren carrying on the annual tradition of the cemetery clean up. And I'm sure they would be happy to tell you many, many more family stories than I included here.

The Family Tree

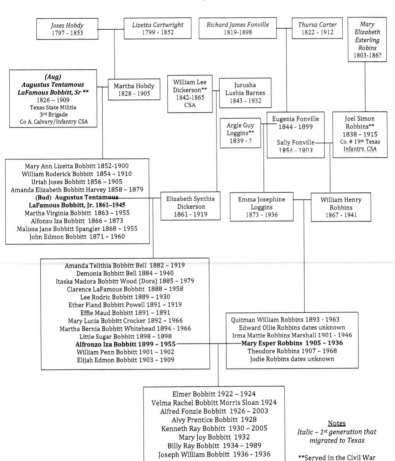

Joses Hobdy 1797 - 1853

Lizetta Cartwright 1799 - 1852

Richard James Fonville 1819-1898

Thursa Carter 1822 - 1912

Mary Elizabeth Esterling Robins 1803-186?

(Aug)
Augustus Tentamous LaFamous Bobbitt, Sr
1826 – 1909
Texas State Militia
3rd Brigade
Co A. Calvary/Infantry CSA

Martha Hobdy 1828 - 1905

William Lee Dickerson**
1842-1865
CSA

Jurusha Lushia Barnes 1843 - 1932

Argle Guy Loggins**
1839 - ?

Eugenia Fonville 1844 - 1899

Sally Fonville 1854 - 1903

Joel Simon Robbins**
1838 – 1915
Co. # 19th Texas Infantry, CSA

Mary Ann Lizetta Bobbitt 1852-1900
William Roderick Bobbitt 1854 – 1910
Uriah Joses Bobbitt 1856 – 1905
Amanda Elizabeth Bobbitt Harvey 1858 – 1879
(Bud) Augustus Tentamous LaFamous Bobbitt, Jr. 1861–1945
Martha Virginia Bobbitt 1863 - 1955
Alfonzo Iza Bobbitt 1866 – 1873
Malissa Jane Bobbitt Spangler 1868 - 1955
John Edmon Bobbitt 1871 - 1960

Elizabeth Synthia Dickerson 1861 - 1919

Emma Josephine Loggins 1873 - 1936

William Henry Robbins 1867 - 1941

Amanda Telithia Bobbitt Bell 1882 – 1919
Demonia Bobbitt Bell 1884 – 1940
Itaska Madora Bobbitt Wood (Dora) 1885 – 1979
Clarence LaFamous Bobbitt 1888 – 1958
Lee Rodric Bobbitt 1889 – 1930
Ether Fland Bobbitt Powell 1891 – 1919
Effie Maud Bobbitt 1891 – 1891
Mary Lucia Bobbitt Crocker 1892 – 1966
Martha Bernia Bobbitt Whitehead 1894 - 1966
Little Sugar Bobbitt 1898 – 1898
Alfronzo Iza Bobbitt 1899 – 1955
William Penn Bobbitt 1901 – 1902
Elijah Edmon Bobbitt 1903 – 1909

Quitman William Robbins 1893 - 1963
Edward Ollie Robbins dates unknown
Irma Mattie Robbins Marshall 1901 - 1946
Mary Esper Robbins 1905 – 1936
Theodore Robbins 1907 – 1968
Jodie Robbins dates unknown

Elmer Bobbitt 1922 – 1924
Velma Rachel Bobbitt Morris Sloan 1924
Alfred Fonzie Bobbitt 1926 – 2003
Alvy Prentice Bobbitt 1928
Kenneth Ray Bobbitt 1930 – 2005
Mary Joy Bobbitt 1932
Billy Ray Bobbitt 1934 – 1989
Joseph William Bobbitt 1936 - 1936

Notes
Italic – 1st generation that migrated to Texas

**Served in the Civil War